Chapter One

THE noise was excruciating.

Two of the more eminent consultants of St Elizabeth's Children's Hospital were startled into disrupting what had been a serious professional discussion.

'What *is* that?' James Fenwick, the top paediatric cardiac surgeon for Lizzie's and probably for Greater London as well, raised a neatly contoured eyebrow.

His companion, the head of the cardiology department, Charles Bruce, tilted his impressive thatch of white hair to one side and then increased his resemblance to Father Christmas by chuckling with amusement.

'*That*, I believe, has to be Kirsty.'

The volume of the awful sound was increasing.

'What can they be doing to the unfortunate child? *Skinning* her?'

Dr Charles Bruce shook his head. 'She's not in pain, James. She's singing.'

James Fenwick raised both eyebrows in an elegant expression of comprehension. 'Is she badly retarded?'

Charles Bruce gave a burst of laughter. 'I hope not. She's one of our new junior staff nurses. From what I've seen in the last week or two, she's going to be a very good one.'

The singing, its enthusiasm matched only by the degree to which it was off key, was terminated abruptly, overpowered by the even louder sound of metallic objects hitting each other with considerable force.

James Fenwick's expression now suggested that Charles may have been a little premature in his positive evaluation. By tacit agreement, both men rounded the corner of the corridor.

'You know my registrar, James? Ian Fraser?'

'Indeed.' James knew the New Zealander quite well. Ian had been on Charles Bruce's team for the better part of a year and his abilities were highly regarded. The surgeon now nodded at the junior doctor who looked suitably embarrassed and promptly stooped to collect the stainless steel trays that had been knocked off the empty meal trolley by the collision.

'Go! Go! Go!' a small voice shrieked into the sudden silence. 'Make it *go!*'

The voice belonged to a tiny child that James Fenwick was well acquainted with. Two-and-a-half-year-old Amy Pennock was one of his Down's syndrome patients. She was due to have her congenital heart defect surgically corrected, by himself in fact, the next morning. As usual, an impish grin lit up the small, round face. Her tiny hands pumped up and down in time to her bouncing as she tried to encourage the fun to continue. 'Go *faster!*' she commanded.

Amy was sitting on a trolley. Or, more correctly, she was bouncing happily within the safely encompassing arms of the nurse who was sitting cross-legged on the trolley. James Fenwick found himself smiling against his better judgement.

'Sorry about the noise, Dr Bruce. Ian's steering was a wee bit off the mark.'

The Scottish accent was pronounced, the inflection of the words a delightful variation on the norm. Ian didn't respond to the accusation. The tall, rather lanky young man looked as though he would like to be whistling and gazing skywards, caught out in a youthful prank but hopeful of being able to disclaim any responsibility. James caught the ghost of a wink that the cardiology consultant directed at his registrar.

'I expect he was a bit distracted by your...ah... singing.'

Charles Bruce was having trouble keeping a straight face and James Fenwick could understand why. The young nurse had the most contagious grin he'd ever seen. It was more mischievous than Amy's and the sparkling blue eyes above it advertised an intelligence the child could never aspire to. The mop of curly red hair that framed the face made James think of clowns. Clowns, circuses and the sheer excitement of being part of it all.

'We've just been taking Amy on a tour up to theatre.' Ian Fraser was doing his best to inject a note of professionalism into the situation. 'Familiarising her with what to expect tomorrow. She seemed apprehensive when I went to check on her earlier.'

'It was my idea to take her up there,' Kirsty volunteered after a quick glance at Ian. 'But Sister said she thought it was a good idea.'

Amy had given up trying to restart her ride. Having stared solemnly at each adult in turn, she struggled to her feet, wrapped her arms firmly around her nurse's neck and planted a resounding kiss on her cheek. James Fenwick's smile widened as he watched the nurse return the kiss with equal enthusiasm.

'You seem to have accomplished your mission.' Charles Bruce's tone suggested that the romp was now over.

Kirsty gave a quick nod. 'Aye, I think it's time we got you back to bed, Moppet.' She climbed off the trolley and gathered the toddler into her arms. 'You're looking forward to your ride tomorrow morning, aren't you, sweetheart?' She returned another affectionate kiss. 'You're going to see the nice man who can fix up your heart, yes?'

'Kirsty...' Charles Bruce was looking amused again '...I'd like you to meet the nice man who can fix up hearts. This is Mr James Fenwick. James, this is Kirsty McTavish.'

'Oh, how do you *do*?' James accepted the hand that appeared from behind Amy's legs and tried to ignore the vague stickiness it imparted. 'I've heard so much about you, Mr Fenwick. Sister said I might be allowed to see part of Amy's surgery tomorrow because I'm not on till the late shift. From the observation room, of course,' she added hastily.

Her enthusiasm was as contagious as her smile.

'You will be most welcome. In fact, why don't you join us *in* theatre? You'll see a lot more that way. We should be kicking off about eight a.m.' His smile was generous. 'I hear you've just joined the staff here at Lizzie's. This will be a good extension of your intro-duction.'

Ian, Kirsty and Amy all moved in the direction of the treatment room which had provided the trolley. Ian was shaking his head at something Kirsty was whis-pering but the only response to his non-verbal admo-nition was a gurgle of laughter. James Fenwick stared thoughtfully at the departing trio.

'I'm not sure why I said that, you know, Charles.' He gave his companion a puzzled glance. 'Do you

ALISON ROBERTS 9

think it's safe to have her loose in my theatre? She's not going to start...singing, or anything, is she?'

'I'll see if we can spare young Ian for a while.' Charles Bruce chuckled again. 'I'll give him instructions to chaperon her a little more effectively this time. Now, what *were* we talking about, James?'

Only Kirsty's legs were visible. The rest of her body was under the bed. Charge Nurse Jane Armstrong knew they were Kirsty's legs. She could think of no other staff member that might be found in quite such a position. The cheerful voice was less muffled as Jane neared the bed.

'So, Goldilocks picked up the spoon to taste Daddy Bear's porridge. Now, William—which pill is going to be Daddy Bear's porridge? This *big* white one?'

A grudging assent was forthcoming, then a scuffling noise and a short silence, followed by an expression of extreme distaste.

'That was yucky,' Kirsty agreed. 'Too cold. So Goldilocks picked up the spoon to try Mummy Bear's porridge. Hang on, William, I've got to get Mummy Bear's porridge into the spoon.' More scuffling sounds ensued and the bed shifted slightly. 'Ooch! The bed bit me!' Kirsty exclaimed.

Jane Armstrong smiled tolerantly as she listened to the child's giggles. She waited until Baby Bear's porridge had been sampled and then watched as Kirsty wriggled backwards and scrambled to her feet. She looked flustered at the sight of Jane.

'Sorry—did you want me for something?'

Jane nodded. 'We've got a new admission coming in. Could you help Ian with it, please? I'll help Anne with the rest of the drug round.' The senior nurse paused. 'Why were you under the bed, Kirsty?'

'William wouldn't come out to take his pills,' Kirsty explained, 'so I took them in to him.' She held out the empty paper cup. 'All done. Record time for William, too.'

Jane shook her head. Why was it that Kirsty McTavish could make the unconventional appear so logical? And how did she manage to change the atmosphere in the whole ward to such a degree that, even after only a couple of weeks, Jane found she was looking forward to when their shifts coincided?

'It's a four-year-old girl coming in,' she informed her junior. 'Jade Reynolds. She's in Room One. Ian's on his way.'

Jade Reynolds' mother looked as washed out as her daughter.

'Try not to worry too much,' Kirsty reassured her. 'Dr Fraser will be here in a minute.' She eyed the fretting child with sympathy. 'Are you not feeling too well, then, darling? Dr Ian will sort you out.'

Jade was not impressed with her new environment. She was even less impressed when 'Dr Ian' arrived. She began crying loudly and buried her face against her mother's shoulder.

Ian Fraser was tired. It was now eight p.m. and he'd been on duty for thirteen hours. Doing an admission of a miserable four-year-old was not an ideal alternative to finally getting some dinner. The cafeteria would probably be closed by the time he was through. He introduced himself briefly, pulling out a chair.

'How old is Jade?' he queried, finding his notebook and pen.

'She was four in March.'

'And what made you bring her in to A and E?'

'She's so tired. She's refused to walk for the last two days. I've had to carry her everywhere.'

'Did it come on suddenly?'

'No. We all had some sort of bug about two weeks ago. Jade's been off her food and tired ever since then. She started coughing about three nights ago.' The woman raised her voice wearily over the sound of her daughter's wails.

Ian sighed inwardly. The examination and chest X-ray done in A and E had shown the possibility of either an enlarged heart or a collection of fluid around the heart. The cause was going to need thorough investigation but the physical examination would not be easy.

He questioned Jade's mother about the child's medical history, which was negative. As he wrote down the details Ian was aware that Jade's crying had stopped suddenly. He looked up to see Kirsty standing behind the child's mother. A fluffy red puppet with wobbly eyes like golf balls was in place on her arm. It appeared from behind the shield of Mrs Reynolds' shoulder as Jade raised her head again.

'Boo!'

Jade hiccuped and then smiled. The puppet disappeared and then popped up again, this time moving forward to tickle Jade's nose. The small girl giggled and Ian felt himself relax noticeably.

'Do you think you could get Jade into bed, Kirsty? I'll come back in a minute to examine her.'

When he returned, he was delighted to find his patient on the bed and out of her mother's arms. Kirsty had draped a stethoscope over the puppet who appeared to be listening to Jade's chest.

'Sounds like a train,' the puppet reported in a squeaky voice with a marked Scottish accent.

'Can I listen, too?' Ian smiled at Jade.

'No,' she responded firmly. 'Only him.' She pointed to the puppet.

'Maybe he can help me,' Ian suggested. He caught Kirsty's delighted grin as she eased her arm out of the puppet. Ian put his own hand inside and made the head nod vigorously. 'I'm going to help Dr Ian. I'm going to hold the round end.'

'That's not how he talks,' Jade complained.

Ian managed to raise his voice an octave. 'Take a big breath, Jade.' He ignored Kirsty's gurgle of laughter at his efforts to mimic her accent. As long as a couple of senior consultants didn't materialise unexpectedly, what did it matter if his dignity went out the window? It seemed to happen quite often around Kirsty McTavish but the job always got done and Ian had to admit that many of his duties were a lot more enjoyable than they used to be.

Even the insertion of a butterfly cannula in the back of Jade's hand to obtain blood samples was accomplished with minimal trauma. Ian left Kirsty to settle the child and her mother in for the night and put in a call to his consultant, Charles Bruce.

'Four-year-old, previously healthy female,' he reported. 'Heart-rate one twenty, respiration twenty, blood pressure ninety over sixty, no fever. Presented with two-week history of fatigue following a viral illness which has got worse over the last few days since she started coughing.' Ian consulted his notes. 'Heart sounds are muffled with a gallop heard at the apex. No murmur. Chest X-ray shows a CTR of seventy-five per cent. Lung fields that can be seen appear normal. Looks like either cardiac enlargement or a pericardial effusion.' He listed the numerous tests the blood had been tagged for.

'Sounds like a viral myocarditis or pericarditis.' Charles confirmed Ian's suspicions. 'Do a twelve lead ECG and call me again. We might need to put her on a monitor. Put a request in for an echocardiogram and a repeat chest X-ray for the morning. Any other problems at the moment?'

'Not yet,' Ian responded. 'But I'm sure something will turn up. I'm on for the night.'

'Good.' Charles Bruce sounded pleased. 'I might get some sleep myself for a change. Keep up the good work, Ian.'

Ian felt more cheerful as he replaced the receiver. It was nice to get some approval, especially having been caught larking around that afternoon by the heads of both the departments he was most closely associated with. That little episode was entirely the fault of Kirsty McTavish, of course. If he didn't enjoy her company so much then her arrival on his ward could have been an absolute disaster.

Kirsty put another two slices of bread into the toaster during her short tea break later that evening. Poor Ian was starving and now he was having to go over Jade Reynolds' ECG with his senior consultant and get some drug therapy initiated. He'd already missed any chance of dinner. She sighed happily as she buttered the slices already cooked. It had been another great day. Fancy being invited into theatre when the famous James Fenwick was operating! She couldn't wait.

Never mind that she wouldn't get to bed until midnight tonight and she would have to be up at the crack of dawn to fit in her run around Regent's Park. She wasn't going to forgo her run. The programme for improving her level of fitness was just as important as the unexpected input into her professional experience.

It was all going exactly to plan. Kirsty smiled to herself, searching the cupboard for some jam or honey to put on the toast. A year ago she would have dreamed of doing precisely what she was doing now. It had seemed, then, that it would remain just that—a dream. She had been trapped, cut off from the nursing career she had loved and the life she had only had a taste of, by her mother's terminal illness.

It had appeared to require only a temporary halt to her career and a period of extended leave from the paediatric position she had gained in her home town of Glasgow shortly after finishing her training at the age of twenty. Kirsty had willingly taken on the task of caring for her much-loved mother and had initially been delighted that the deterioration in her condition had been so slow. It had become a way of life. A routine that had been comforting in its familiarity. As comforting as her mother had found the stories of romance and happy endings that Kirsty had faithfully collected from the library for her each week and later read aloud as her mother's eyesight had failed. Her mother's life had been hard and the ending had been far from perfect but she had retained her faith in an ideal that she could experience herself through fantasy. Kirsty had obliged happily. She had given as much as she could to improve the quality of her only parent's remaining life and had kept her own frustrations well buried. It hadn't been until the death of her mother more than three years later that Kirsty had realised just how much of her own life had been put on hold. Her mother's release had been a relief to both of them in the end but suddenly Kirsty had found her life had been totally empty. She'd had no family, no job and very little money. And she'd probably been the only twenty-four-year-old virgin within the Scottish borders!

The advanced paediatric nursing course in London had been the light at the end of a mercifully short tunnel. The last of her small inheritance had gone on the fees for the intensive six-month course. Her optimism about gaining a position at the completion of the course had been well founded. Kirsty had started at St Elizabeth's Children's Hospital only two weeks later. The cardiology ward might not have been her first choice but the availability of a room in the staff quarters had made the decision easy. The cost of living in London was horrendous! It was only a beginning, after all. A beginning of a *real* life!

It was the smoke from the toaster that brought Kirsty out of her brown study. The smoke and the sudden entrance of an alarmed Ian Fraser.

'Are you trying to burn the place down, Kirsty McTavish?'

'No.' Kirsty was offended. 'I was making *you* some toast. I thought you might be hungry.'

'I am. Starving!' Ian eyed the still-smouldering squares that Kirsty had flipped into the sink. 'Charcoal's carcinogenic, but what the hell? I haven't eaten since lunch.'

'I've made some more. Here.' Kirsty passed him the plate. 'Would you like a cup of tea?'

'Coffee, please. Black. You're an angel of mercy, Kirsty. I take back everything I said this afternoon.'

Kirsty busied herself and made a pot of tea at the

same time. One of the senior nurses, Anne, paused by the kitchen door, carrying a crying child.

'Pour me one, would you, please, Kirsty? I'm just going to ferry Shannon along the corridor for a minute to see if I can settle her. Otherwise we'll have to hit the Phenergan, I think. Her mum's had enough for one day.'

'Kirsty could sing her a lullaby,' Ian offered through a large mouthful of toast.

'Thanks, Ian.' Anne's look was not appreciative. 'I owe you one.'

Kirsty hadn't missed the byplay. 'Some children have been known to fall asleep instantly when I sing to them,' she informed Ian as Anne moved away.

'Probably feigning death. It's a good escape route.' Ian grinned.

'So...Pavarotti.' Kirsty's eyes narrowed dramatically over the rim of her teacup. 'What was that dulcet wee sound I heard coming from your room last night, then?'

Ian reached for his coffee. 'I was practising. On my chanter.'

'Excuse me?'

'It's kind of a part of the bagpipes. The pipe thing. The practice chanter's a bit quieter than using the whole set-up with the drones and bag. You should know. You're a lot more Scottish than I am.'

'I'm beginning to wonder. Where was it you said you came from again?'

'Dunedin. In the South Island of New Zealand. They call it the "Little Edinburgh." Predominantly Scottish settlers including my great-grandparents. Lots of old stone buildings and awful weather. You'd love it.'

'I don't think so.' Kirsty rolled her eyes. 'I've just

managed to escape. I plan to start *really* living. I intend to find somewhere sunny, with great food and even better wine. I want music. *Real* music—not someone in a tartan skirt, standing on a lonely hill and squashing a dying cat.'

'That's rich—coming from you,' Ian muttered but he was laughing. 'What else do you want, Kirsty? Or should I say "Kusty"?' He was still grinning. 'I love the way you say your name. Do you think I could pick up a Scottish accent while I'm here?'

'I wouldn't bother.' Kirsty returned the grin. 'Yours is quite horrible enough the way it is.'

It was Ian's turn to roll his eyes. For a moment they were silent, alone in a corner of the kitchen that was positioned in a central area of a large ward, now getting well settled for the night. The corridor lights were dimmed, the occasional cries of children muted. Ian was on the point of enquiring hopefully about the possibility of some more toast when Kirsty spoke softly.

'You know what I really want, Ian?' She didn't wait for his response. 'I want to fall in love. A grand, passionate romance.' Kirsty thought of an amalgam of all the heroes of her mother's stories and sighed rather wistfully. 'I want to be swept off my feet and carried into the future by someone so exciting I wouldn't be able to resist. I'm twenty-four and that's never happened yet.'

'Well, I'm twenty-eight and it's not something I expect to find around the next corner.'

'No.' Kirsty's face was solemn now. 'You know what our problem is, Ian?'

'No, what?' Ian's answer coincided with his beep sounding.

'Our problem is—we've both got red hair.'

Ian reached for the phone. 'Speak for yourself, Kirsty McTavish. Mine's definitely auburn.'

Kirsty was uncharacteristically silent as they took the lift to the top floor of Lizzie's.

'Now remember. You're not to touch anything, or talk to anyone. And, for God's sake, don't even *think* about singing.'

Kirsty sniffed and tried to look highly offended but she couldn't keep it up. Her excitement bubbled over when the lift doors finally opened.

'Come *on*, Ian! They'll be finished before we even get there.'

'I doubt it,' Ian said dryly. 'It is quite a long procedure. No, come this way, Kirsty. We've got to get some theatre gear on first.'

She looked like a child playing at dress-ups. The theatre gown was the wrong size. It came right down to the elasticised booties covering her shoes but Kirsty was too impatient to change. The hat also looked too big, puffed out by the wealth of curls it rested on. When the mask was tied, only an enormous pair of blue eyes and a dusting of freckles on the bridge of Kirsty's nose were showing. And she still managed to look more attractive than any woman Ian had ever come across.

He needn't have worried about her behaviour. Nurse McTavish was clearly overawed by their environment. Theatre was staffed to the hilt. Two surgeons, an anaesthetist, registrars, several technicians and a full complement of nursing staff. James Fenwick acknowledged their entrance but no other introductions were made. Kirsty and Ian were invited to stand on a small platform at the head of the table tucked in behind the bank of anaesthetic equipment. It was a privileged position for spectators, allowing the clearest view of the whole operating field without being in the way of anyone involved in the procedure.

Ian knew that Kirsty had only been in a theatre briefly, during her nursing training. She had been fascinated but not attracted to take her career in that direction.

'Too rigid,' she had explained. 'Not nearly enough scope for using any imagination.'

He wondered now how she would cope, observing major surgery on a child he knew she had quickly formed a deep attachment for. Sure enough, as Amy's tiny chest was opened and the cruel looking rib spreaders were positioned, he heard her quick intake of breath and saw what was visible of her face go pale, making her freckles stand out much more noticeably. Ian reached for her hand and found the grip returned tightly with obvious gratitude. After that, it seemed quite natural to stand there, holding hands, out of place and yet feeling central to a drama that was unfolding around them.

Activity in the theatre slowed after the cannulae for bypass were inserted. James Fenwick stood back a little and glanced up at his small audience.

'We're cooling down,' he explained. 'It'll take another twenty minutes or so. The bypass unit has an oxygenator and a heat exchanger. We measure the nasopharyngeal temperature because that's the nearest measurable point to the brain. When that gets down to about twenty degrees centigrade we'll clamp the aorta and get started. Do you know what Amy's problem is, Kirsty?'

She nodded. 'Amy has a medium-sized ventricular septal defect.'

'And do you know why this surgery wasn't done when she was an infant?'

Kirsty shook her head and squeezed Ian's hand. He answered for her.

'Amy's parents weighed up the risks and elected to have medical rather than surgical treatment. They hoped the defect would decrease and then close spontaneously.'

James Fenwick nodded. 'But it hasn't. There's been no decrease in size and she still shows an enlarged heart and pulmonary plethora.'

'She's had trouble with recurrent chest infections requiring hospital admissions and has needed treatment for heart failure on two occasions,' Ian added quietly as James turned his attention back to his tiny patient. 'Now her exercise tolerance has decreased even more and she tires very easily.'

Kirsty nodded. 'She was sound asleep before I even got her back to bed yesterday,' she whispered.

Theatre staff were becoming more active again.

'We're going to clamp the aorta now,' James Fenwick explained. 'We'll perfuse a solution of ice-cold Ringer's containing an excess of potassium into the coronary arteries via the root of the aorta.'

Amy's heart stopped beating instantly. The surgeons seemed to speak only to each other after that. The nurses and technical staff quietly responded to orders and attended to their own duties. Ian and Kirsty watched, both highly impressed with the surgeons' skill as they meticulously repaired what seemed like a tiny defect in the wall separating the two larger chambers of the miniature heart. When the repair was complete,

the atmosphere became more relaxed as Amy's body
was rewarmed slowly. The heart eventually began beating again unassisted.

'Right. Let's get this lass off bypass.' James Fenwick
glanced up at Kirsty once again. 'You should have her
back on the ward by tomorrow. She'll probably be up
and around within a day or two.'

James Fenwick's predictions were as good as his surgery. Ian still found it astonishing the way children
could bounce back after such major surgery. Amy was
not only recovering from the surgery with remarkable
rapidity, she was actually making progress towards a
milestone that was well overdue by normal standards.
It had been Kirsty who had encouraged the child, previously reluctant even to stand, into taking her first
steps as part of her mobilisation programme. Now, at
only seven days post-surgery, arrangements for Amy
Pennock's discharge were well under way. Kirsty's optimism, patience and affectionate persistence would
have to find another target.

Not that that would be difficult. She was also Jade
Reynolds' favourite nurse, especially when 'Mr Red'
the fluffy puppet was attached to her arm. But Jade
was also due for discharge, probably today, after a
seven-day stay in hospital. The diagnosis of viral myocarditis was a serious one but Jade had responded well
to therapy so far. Her heart function had improved
though it was still far from normal. She was to be discharged on a maintenance dose of digoxin and Lasix
to control the heart rhythm and fluid retention. Her
activities would also need to remain restricted and
she would be checked at an outpatient clinic in two
weeks' time.

So, neither of these young girls would be the lucky recipient of Nurse McTavish's attention for much longer. That still left an entire ward full of responsive youngsters—and one not so young. Ian Fraser had noticed with considerable pleasure that Kirsty's duty roster had shifted from late to early duties. As most of his time was spent in or near the ward that meant he would be seeing a lot more of her.

Ian had never met anyone, male or female, with whom it had been so easy to strike up a good friendship. Both of them living in the staff quarters helped the rapport, as did working in the same department. They also shared a commitment to keep fit and, while Ian had had to slow his pace the first time he had come across her running in Regent's Park, she could almost match his speed now for short distances. But the friendship went far deeper than that.

In Ian's opinion, they were a perfect match. Two sides of the same coin. He brought some maturity to play against Kirsty's impulsiveness. Her vivacity chased away his more sombre outlook on life. They shared an almost identical sense of humour and enjoyed the competition of seeing who could make the other laugh more. Kirsty couldn't sing but that didn't dampen her enthusiasm at all which was actually more comprehensible to Ian than he let on. He couldn't play the bagpipes but he had still carried the bulky instrument halfway across the world with him. They both even had red hair!

It was easy to coast along simply enjoying the relationship they had established but Ian wanted to give it a nudge. He was going to ask Kirsty out and make it clear, somehow, that their friendship had the potential to become much more meaningful. Heading into the ward to prepare for the morning ward round, Ian found himself looking for Kirsty. She should have come on duty an hour ago but she was nowhere to be seen. Then he heard the squeals of glee and loud splashing noises emanating from the ward bathroom. Sure enough, Kirsty's distinctive gurgle of laughter was mixed into the cacophony of sounds. Ian cast an eye around. If the charge nurse found too much water on the floor then Kirsty would be in trouble—and not for the first time.

None of the senior nursing staff was immediately visible but Ian hovered, as though standing guard. He was beside the large notice-board that posted copies of duty rosters as well as a collection of children's art-work, cards from grateful families and photographs of previous patients. It was quite a legitimate position to stand for a minute or two but Ian turned almost guiltily as someone approached. He relaxed instantly. There was no need to warn Kirsty. The newcomer posed no threat to the current romp going on in the bathroom.

'Paolo! How's it going? I didn't know you were back.'

'*Ciao*, Ian.' A lazy smile lifted the corners of Paolo Tonolo's mouth. 'I got back only last night.'

'Did you have a good holiday?'

'It was not a holiday, *amico mio*. My grandmother was very ill.' Paolo's smile suddenly broadened and he dropped an almost imperceptible wink. 'A cruise on my father's yacht did wonders for her convalescence.' Paolo peered at the duty roster on the notice-board.

Ian shook his head. Paolo was incorrigible. He appeared to be part of a very unhealthy family that required frequent visits back to his native Italy. But who could blame him? If Ian was the favoured younger son of an enormously wealthy Italian family he would probably want to take advantage of the opportunities it provided as well. It wasn't as if Paolo needed a career. He was doing it out of personal interest. What did irk Ian slightly was that he could have such a totally relaxed attitude to something like a career as a cardiac surgeon and still be good at what he did.

Paolo was James Fenwick's senior registrar and he was good enough for even the head of department to tolerate his regular absences. Aside from his abilities, thanks to family connections, Paolo slotted neatly into James Fenwick's social circle as well. Paolo had been educated and trained in London; his accent and lapses into Italian were purely for effect. And they were effective. Ian genuinely liked his colleague. Nobody could fail to fall under Paolo's spell.

The naked toddler that darted out of the bathroom door and ran behind the two men drew their attention instantly.

'Victoria! Come back here!' Kirsty McTavish also burst out of the bathroom door. Damp red curls clung to her face. The white shirt of her uniform was clinging to her body in a way the designer had certainly not intended it to, thanks to the large wet areas and the fact that Kirsty had forgotten to don her apron. Victoria had reached the door of her room. Her grinning face was just visible as she waited for Kirsty's pursuit to continue.

But Kirsty had stopped in her tracks. Her silence gave Ian his first twinge of alarm.

'Kirsty? You won't have met Paolo, yet. He's been on leave. Paolo is James Fenwick's senior surgical registrar.'

Ian was watching Kirsty's face as he made the in-

troduction. He registered the peculiar stillness of her
normally mobile features with increasing dismay. Even
though her face was transfixed, Kirsty's hand had come
out with her customary friendly overture. The response
was more than she had anticipated. The surgical registrar took the small, sturdy hand as though accepting
a fragile gift. Then he raised it to his lips.

'*Ciao*. Paolo,' he murmured.

She couldn't possibly fall for it, Ian told himself. It
was so blatant! And what could Paolo have seen in
Kirsty that had brought the continental charm out in
full force? She was nothing like the type of women Ian
had seen him with. Kirsty was far too young…far too
innocent. Ian's heart dived several more notches as he
watched her lips curve in delight and her eyes dance.
She *had* fallen for it. She made no attempt to withdraw
her hand or break the eye contact they were locked
into.

'I'm very pleased to meet you, Paulo. I'm Kirsty
McTavish.'

'No, no, no.' Paolo shook his head sorrowfully as he
finally released her hand. 'Not Paul-o. Pay-*oh*-lo.'

'Pay-*oh*-lo,' Kirsty repeated obediently. Then she
grinned. '*Ciao*, Paolo.'

They hadn't stopped staring at each other. Ian felt
quite invisible. He breathed a sigh of relief as Paolo
Tonolo's beep sounded and the registrar walked away
with an apologetic '*Scusi*' and an overdone expression
of regret. Surely now the spell would be broken and
Kirsty would be able to see that Paolo had merely been
amusing himself?

She was staring after him. She didn't even seem to
notice that he had passed young Victoria, still stark
naked, dancing in the corridor under the astonished

gaze of the charge nurse. Then her gaze shifted back to Ian and he knew there was absolutely no hope for him. Kirsty McTavish had just been swept very firmly off her feet. Even now her eyes were not entirely focused on him.

'Is he real?' she asked solemnly. 'Or did I just dream the whole thing?'

'Don't ask me,' Ian responded glumly. 'I think I just ceased to exist.'

Chapter Two

'I'LL have to get some high heels.'

'I wouldn't advise it.' Ian Fraser could feel his sweat-soaked T-shirt clinging to his back. He slowed his pace as Kirsty shouted her question for the second time.

'I said, why not?'

'You'd look silly.' Ian dropped his pace to a slow jog to let Kirsty catch up. They had done their circuit of the zoo's perimeter and were now following the canal, parallel to Prince Albert Road. The morning's run was almost over. Ian looked over his shoulder at Kirsty. 'And you'd never keep up with me—running in high heels.'

Kirsty managed to laugh, but only just. She was well out of breath. She stopped and flopped onto the grass, then she flung herself onto her back, arms outstretched.

'I wasn't planning to *run* in them, Jimmy! I just thought they'd make my legs look skinnier.'

Ian leaned against the trunk of an ancient tree, welcoming its shade, gently stretching his calf muscles. 'There's nothing wrong with your legs.'

'Maybe I'll dye my hair, then. Jet black.'

'Yeah, right.' Ian towered over Kirsty, extending his hand. 'Come on, up you get. We'd better go and catch a shower and breakfast. I've got to get to work.'

'Me, too.' Kirsty allowed Ian to pull her to her feet, checking her watch as he let go of her hand. 'Oh, hell! I've only got half an hour.'

27

She started towards the road at a brisk walk. 'I'll have to skip breakfast. That's good—it'll cut down a few calories.'

'It's not good,' Ian growled. 'And why are you so worried about what you look like all of a sudden?'

Kirsty was silent and Ian knew the answer only too well anyway. He decided to bite the bullet and get Kirsty's preoccupation finally aired.

'Why don't you ask *him* out, if you're so keen?'

'Oh, I couldn't do that!' Kirsty was horrified.

'Why not? I thought women were allowed to do that sort of thing these days. Taking the initiative should be right up your street.'

'It just wouldn't be...it's not...' Kirsty's face was twisted into lines of deep frustration.

'Romantic enough?' Ian finished for her.

'Exactly.' Kirsty's grin was embarrassed. 'I want him to notice *me*. I don't want to have to dangle a sign in front of him.' Kirsty sighed heavily. 'He's never around enough. I've hardly seen him for a week and when he's on the ward I'm always busy. I think those children throw up and fill their nappies on purpose. What am I going to do, Ian? I'm getting desperate!'

It was Ian's turn to sigh heavily. He had been re-lieved that Paolo Tonolo had not followed up the in-terest Ian had been sure he'd detected when he'd intro-duced him to Kirsty. Any hope that Kirsty's infatuation would fade had been dispelled by an increasing fre-quency of asking questions about the registrar and de-preciative comments about her own appearance. Now Kirsty wanted his help to send her into the arms of another man. And because he cared so much about her, Ian was resigned to the knowledge that her happiness would have to override his own inclinations.

'There's a pub that a lot of the staff hang out in in the evenings. Paolo goes there quite often. I'll take you tonight if you like.'

'Oh, Ian!' Kirsty had been two steps ahead of him, almost onto the pedestrian crossing despite the red light. She whirled suddenly and flung her arms around Ian, standing on tiptoes to plant an enthusiastic kiss on his cheek. 'You're an angel!' she cried. 'I *love* you!'

Ian's smile was poignant but Kirsty didn't notice. The lights had changed and she was already heading rapidly across the road towards Lizzie's staff quarters. Ian had dreamed of hearing exactly those words and of being kissed by Kirsty McTavish but the reality pushed his dream even further away. He was cast firmly into the role of a friend. Worse, a big brother, to whom physical affection could be expressed with no fear of misinterpretation. It was as close as he'd been able to get but it was far too far away to satisfy Ian.

Kirsty still felt overheated from her run despite the cool shower. Having to rush to get onto the ward in time hadn't helped but it had been the sight of Paolo Tonolo at the far end of the ward that had really negated the effect of the shower.

He had to be the most gorgeous male creature she had ever seen. He was as tall as Ian but much broader across the shoulders and he moved with the languid grace of a large cat, sculptured muscles encased in smooth, olive-brown skin. Jet-black, straight hair sat perfectly—probably aided by a bit of mousse, Kirsty suspected, but the idea of a man caring for his appearance to that degree was not the least off-putting. Tall, dark and unbelievably handsome, Paolo had stepped straight from the pages of a plot her mother would have loved. He was also rich. Ian had told her about the family yacht, their famous art collection, their castle in Tuscany. It was as exotic as it could be. Like his accent and his jewellery—the tiny gold cross that hung around his neck and the gold signet ring on the third finger of his right hand.

The sight of those hands was enough to send shivers up Kirsty's spine. The fantasies she had conjured up during the restless nights of the previous week had led her to believe she knew exactly what the effect of those long, elegant fingers would be if they came in contact with her body. But it was his eyes that could knock the breath right out of her lungs. As black as his hair, they appeared to have the ability to caress as physically as his hands had the potential to do. During that first, too brief introduction, Kirsty had felt his gaze stroke her body. She had also felt, for the first time in her life, the ignition of a desire that was actually physically painful in its intensity. She had always thought that going wobbly around the knees was purely the stuff of romantic fiction, but when those lips had pressed lingeringly against her hand Kirsty had known that it was a genuine phenomenon.

Everything about Paolo Tonolo was perfect. Except for one thing. He was not interested in her. Sure, he had appeared smitten when they'd been introduced and Kirsty had felt, only too effectively, the long glances he'd bestowed in her direction when their orbits had crossed in the ward, but he had done nothing to follow it up. Kirsty was ready. *More* than ready but she wasn't going to take the first step. That didn't happen in the books and her first romance had to be perfect. She had waited too long to settle for anything less.

Kirsty knew that Paolo's brief round would include

one of the patients on her own list for the day so she made young Harry Wilton her first priority. Harry was seven years old, an intelligent, serious child who was facing a major procedure that day with great courage. Harry had contracted Kawasaki disease as a two-year-old. The severe illness had damaged the arteries in his heart enough for him to have suffered a heart attack as a three-year-old.

The severe scar formation and narrowing of his main coronary artery had made the small child a semi-invalid, living with the management of his heart failure the predominant focus of his life. Now the deterioration in Harry's condition had prompted the surgeons to consider a coronary artery bypass procedure. The final decision on surgery was waiting for the results of a cardiac catheterisation test that Ian Fraser was going to perform this morning.

Harry was sitting on his bed, looking solemn, as usual. A very battered panda bear lay beside him and he was reading a 'Goosebumps' story. Kirsty put her arm around his shoulders.

'*The Blob That Ate Everyone*. Sounds good!'

'It's smashing! This kid is writing a story and everything he writes is coming true. He's just put a Blob Monster in his basement and its waiting for *fresh meat*!'

'Ooh!' Kirsty looked appropriately scared. 'Where's Mum and Dad?'

'They went to get some breakfast.'

'OK. Sorry you can't have any, Harry.'

'That's all right. I'll have a big lunch. Mum said she'd go and get me a hamburger and chips.'

'Fantastic.' Kirsty licked her lips. 'Maybe she could get me one, too.' Missing breakfast hadn't been such a good idea. Kirsty could feel her stomach growling already. 'I'm starving.'

'Me, too.'

'Well, I've got something for you to swallow.'

'What is it?'

'Medicine.' Kirsty held out the hollow-handled spoon containing the dose of Demerol and Phenergan. 'It makes you a bit sleepy so you won't feel too nervous.'

'A sedative.' Harry gave Kirsty a slightly exasperated look that made her laugh.

'OK, smarty-pants. Is there anything else you want to know about having the catheter test?'

'No. Dr Ian told me all about it yesterday.' Harry fished around in the clutter on top of his bedside cabinet. 'Look, he even gave me an old catheter to look at.' Harry held up the long, flexible plastic tubing. 'It's long, isn't it?'

'It's got to go all the way from the top of your leg into your heart.'

'It goes into my femoral artery. Just here.' Harry prodded his groin with his forefinger importantly. 'And when it gets to my heart then I get shoved full of radioactive stuff so everything glows when they want to take pictures.'

'Something like that.' Kirsty smiled. 'The contrast material will show up the arteries and veins in your heart. I don't think you'll light up the whole cath lab with a green glow or anything, though.'

'Oh.' Harry looked disappointed. Then he sighed heavily.

'Are you worried, Harry?' Kirsty tipped her head sideways to peer into the small, downcast face. 'Panda can go with you, you know. And you can take *The Blob That Ate Everyone*. Someone will read it to you.'

'I'll be finished it by then.'

'Take another one. You've got half a bookshop under your bed.' Kirsty pulled out a cardboard box. 'What about *The Deadly Experiments of Dr Eeek*?'

'Will you come and read it to me? Mum and Dad aren't allowed to come in.'

'I'm not sure I'd be allowed to either,' Kirsty warned, 'but I'll ask the boss.'

'Allowed to what?' Kirsty's heart gave a violent flutter at the accented voice close behind her. She turned to find Paolo and Ian both gazing at her. Paolo looked intrigued. Ian looked worried.

'I want Kirsty to come with me when I have my catheter test,' Harry announced.

Ian looked dubious. 'Kirsty's pretty busy here on the ward, Harry. We'll look after you. There's lots of nice nurses in the cath lab.'

Harry's bottom lip protruded. 'I'm not going without Kirsty. She's the nicest nurse.'

'If I was Harry, I would also wish for Kirsty to hold my hand.' Paolo's eyes were doing it to her again. Kirsty forced herself to take a long, steadying breath. 'Surely you can arrange for this small thing, Ian?'

Ian was now looking resigned. 'I'll talk to Jane but only on one condition, Kirsty.'

'What's that?'

'That you don't start singing.'

'You can sing, Kirsty?' Paolo's gaze had the effect of a laser beam. Kirsty could feel tingles in places where she hadn't even been aware she had places. 'I love to sing also. Do you like opera?'

'Kirsty can shatter glasses even when she hums,

Paolo.' Ian turned away. 'I'll go and have a word with Jane. See you soon, Harry.'

Paolo followed his colleague out of the room. Harry was staring at Kirsty.

'What did he mean, you can shatter glasses?'

'He was being very rude.' Kirsty grinned. 'He just doesn't like my singing.'

'Why not?'

'Goodness knows. I'm not that terrible.'

'Sing something,' Harry commanded.

'OK. As long as you sing it with me. Do you know "It's A Long Way To Tipperary"?'

'No.' Harry yawned suddenly, the effects of the sedative becoming apparent.

'I'll teach it to you—if you don't fall asleep on me first.'

As Kirsty and Harry sang goodbye to Piccadilly and bade farewell to Leicester Square, Ian groaned. 'Oh, God, we should have given Kirsty the Demerol.'

One of the cath lab nurses giggled. The radiographer made a show of clapping her hands over her ears as Kirsty and Harry sang that it was a long way to Tipperary.

'Hey, Harry.' Ian leaned over his small patient. 'You might feel a wee bit of pushing now while we get this tube into the right place. Are you OK?'

Harry nodded but didn't stop singing, declaring his heart was right there.

'So it is,' Ian agreed. 'Let's have an X-ray and make sure the catheter's right there as well.'

Kirsty and Harry both watched the screen as the fluoroscope traced the tip of the catheter as it moved towards the heart.

'It looks like a worm,' Harry decided. The tip began jerking as it entered the heart.

'A worm with hiccups,' Kirsty agreed. 'Or maybe something from one of Dr Eeek's experiments.'

The procedure was time-consuming as a map of Harry's cardiac circulation was documented and various measurements recorded. Kirsty turned to their supplies of distraction materials as Harry became more bored. His fear of the large machines had faded by the time they had finished their first song. *Dr Eeek* was an interactive book, an excellent choice for distraction. Kirsty soon had Harry facing ten-foot-long Komodo dragons about to shred him with their jagged teeth.

'Do you freeze on page seventy-five?' she queried. 'Or run like crazy to page eighty-six?'

'Run like crazy,' Harry decided. 'I'm not stupid.'

Kirsty flicked over to page eighty-six and continued the chase with the Komodo dragons. She managed to keep one eye on the fluoroscopy screen, however, and her heart sank when she saw the degree of damage to Harry's main coronary artery. It looked as though surgery was going to be the only viable option.

Within an hour of the cardiac catheterisation procedure, both Harry's parents went to a conference with Charles Bruce, James Fenwick, Paolo and Ian.

'They're going to talk about me, aren't they?' Harry asked Kirsty.

'You're the most important thing we all have to talk about at the moment.' Kirsty had her hand on Harry's wrist, the other hand holding out the fob watch pinned to her shirt. 'Be quiet for a wee bit, sweetheart. I've got to take your pulse for a whole minute.'

'You've just done it,' Harry grumbled.

Kirsty didn't respond until she had completed the

count. 'I've got to do it every fifteen minutes for a while. Now I'm going to take your blood pressure again, too.' Kirsty charted the results with satisfaction. No cardiac arrhythmias noted and no fall in blood pressure that might indicate bleeding from a cardiac perforation or the arterial entry site. The pulse in Harry's foot was still weaker on the side of entry but the colour and temperature of the extremity was good and there was no sign of oozing from the puncture site.

'Do you feel like that hamburger yet?'

'No. I feel sick.'

'That's probably because of the contrast material in your blood. I'll get you a glass of ice chips and you can suck on those. It might help.'

'Am I going to have to have an operation?' Harry's eyes filled with tears and Kirsty's heart was wrenched as she saw him pull his battered panda bear closer.

'I don't know, love.' Kirsty hugged the small boy. 'I do know that we all want to make you as well as we possibly can. If an operation is going to do that then it will be worth it, won't it?' Kirsty rubbed Harry's head gently. 'Do you know, I don't think an operation would be as scary as what you did this morning.'

'Why not?'

'Well, you'd be asleep. You were awake for the catheter and you coped brilliantly. Even when I was singing.'

'I like your singing,' Harry declared stoutly. 'Will you sing something now?'

'I'll just go and fetch the ice for you first. You think up a song while I'm gone.'

* * *

'It just seems far too young to be having bypass surgery.' Kirsty sighed. 'He's such a neat kid.'

'His odds without the surgery aren't great.' Ian smiled at Kirsty's anxious expression. 'He may do very well. Stop worrying about him—we're almost there. See? That's the pub just along the road.'

Kirsty slowed her pace. 'Are you sure this is a good idea, Ian?'

No, Ian wanted to say. It was the worst idea he'd ever had in his life. Instead, he smiled and nodded reassuringly. 'It's a great idea. I'm in dire need of a beer. It's been a long day.'

'But...' Kirsty had stopped completely '...do I look all right?'

Ian had to grit his teeth as he once again took in the transformation Kirsty had effected since she'd gone off duty that afternoon. Make-up had covered her freckles and darkened her eyelashes and lids but it was not overdone. The pale lipstick made her mouth look as soft as the fabric of her summery dress. Her eyeshadow mirrored the moss-green shade that was a perfect foil for her colouring. Kirsty looked stunning, like some woodland creature emerging from a forest in spring. She also looked younger and more feminine than Ian had ever acknowledged. It aroused a protective instinct that made him feel distinctly grumpy. He should not be doing this. In Ian's opinion, it was tantamount to plonking a shot of whisky in front of an alcoholic.

'You look fine,' he muttered. 'Come on. Let's get this over with.'

Ian sat Kirsty at a corner table and went to the bar to get them both a drink. Paolo was standing at the bar with a group of Lizzie's younger medical staff.

'Ian! Come and join us.'

'I've got Kirsty with me.' Ian's head tilted to indicate the corner table and Paolo's gaze shifted smoothly.

'Ah!' Dark eyes regarded Ian again; an eyebrow lifted. 'She is your girlfriend, no?'

'No.' Ian's reply was terse. He finally caught the attention of the barmaid. 'A pint and a glass of white wine, please.' He didn't look back at Paolo. 'Kirsty would prefer to look elsewhere.' Why did he have to be so damned honest? Ian could have put a stop to this whole charade right then. Instead, he had just offered Kirsty up on a plate.

Paolo's outward breath was an expression in itself. 'She is so...'

'Young?' Ian offered bluntly. He counted out some coins to pay for the drinks. 'Innocent?'

'Ah, yes. *Ingènua*. She's *adoràbile*.'

'And vulnerable.' Ian knew Kirsty was watching them. It was a last stand on his part. 'She could be very easily hurt, Paolo.'

'I would never do that, Ian.' Paolo's tone suggested a severe injury to his ego. He drained the last of his wine. 'I think Kirsty wants something I am only too happy to offer.'

'You could be right.' Ian glanced back towards the corner table and his heart gave a painful lurch. Kirsty was doing her best to appear nonchalant and controlled but her expression was as good as a placard. And the message did not have his name on it.

Paolo snapped his fingers and gained the instant, smiling attention of the barmaid. 'A bottle of chilled champagne, please,' he ordered. 'And two glasses.'

Ian wondered if he could get a refund on the glass of white wine. It appeared to be as redundant as he was himself now. He remained with the group at the bar

but didn't stay more than an hour. The general atmosphere within the group of Lizzie's staff only rein-
forced his own bleakness. Mark Summers and Kate
Lamb were amongst the group. Ian was aware that the
two anaesthetists had been living together since June.
Now the couple were radiating happiness over the news
that Kate's pregnancy had just been confirmed. It
seemed that nobody wanted to talk of anything other
than the wedding plans and the excitement of becoming
parents for the first time. Ian's gaze refused to stray
from the pair at the corner table for more than a minute
or two at a time and Kirsty's gurgles of laughter cut
through the background noise of the pub like some sort
of alarm system.

Ian's room was too far away from Kirsty's on their
floor of the staff quarters for him to have any idea
about what time she came back. Apparently it had been
too late for her to get up in time for their run through
Regent's Park. Or perhaps she hadn't made it back at
all? Ian had been to a party once at Paolo's exclusive
Chelsea address. The town house belonged to his family but most of the time Paolo had it to himself. The
live-in staff occupied the discreet basement level and
Ian could be sure the master bed was always turned
back invitingly and chilled champagne could be available at a moment's notice.

Ian started the day in a bad mood. He was quite
ready to find fault with whatever Kirsty was doing. He
needed the opportunity to snipe at her to relieve his
own feelings but, faced with her glow of happiness and
ecstatic smile as she replaced case-note folders into the
cart, Ian could only shake his head and smile back.

'Was it as good as you hoped for, then?'

'Better!' Kirsty breathed reverently. 'Paolo's got

tickets for a show in the weekend. He's asked me to go with him.'

'A date!' Ian tried to look encouraging.

'And he asked *me*!' Kirsty looked as though she couldn't believe her luck.

'What's the show?'

'He said it in Italian. I can't remember.' Kirsty shrugged. 'It's out of the city a bit. At a place called Glyndebourne. Maybe it's got a good stadium for rock concerts.'

Ian smothered a laugh. 'I come from the other side of the world and even I know you don't go to rock concerts at Glyndebourne.'

'What do they have there?'

'Opera.' Ian was beginning to feel more cheerful. 'Fur coats and strings of pearls and glasses shattering all over the place. It's perfect for you.'

Kirsty looked downcast. 'You mean I don't get to dance?'

Ian grinned. 'You can if you want to but I imagine it would be a first for Glyndebourne.'

Kirsty glanced over her shoulder. 'Listen, Ian, don't tell Paolo, but...I can't *stand* opera singing.'

Ian felt great. 'I won't breathe a word.' Looking away from Kirsty as she slotted the last set of case notes into place, Ian found the ideal person to direct his happy smile towards. 'Crystal! What a nice surprise. Have you met Kirsty?'

'No, I haven't. Hello, Kirsty.'

Kirsty was eyeing the unusual items Crystal was carrying. 'Hi, Crystal. Looks like your spoon has had a nasty accident.'

Ian laughed. 'Crystal's an occupational therapist in

our paediatric rheumatology unit. I spent some time down there before I started on cardiology.'

'Oh.' Kirsty nodded. 'Did you bring those for Emma?'

'Yes.' Crystal looked worriedly at Ian. 'How is she?'

'It *is* rheumatoid pericarditis. I think we're getting things under control. Her hands have got a lot worse, though, haven't they?'

Crystal nodded. 'Peter's got her lined up for more surgery when she gets over this complication.'

'How is Peter?'

'Working too hard, as usual.'

'Crystal's husband Peter's a surgeon here,' Ian explained to Kirsty. 'They were both very kind to me when I first arrived.' Ian's beep sounded. 'Sorry, I'll have to get that. Kirsty, can you take Crystal to see Emma?'

'Sure, she's in Room Three. This way.'

'How's Nikki?' Ian called after them. 'And David?'

'Great,' Crystal answered. 'They love Sydney. They're thinking of a visit soon.'

Ian was back a few minutes later. He beckoned Kirsty away from watching Crystal demonstrate the adapted cutlery to twelve-year-old Emma.

'I need you to come and help me with an admission. An eighteen-month-old boy being transferred from General Medicine. He was admitted with what they thought was a severe dose of measles but Ben Harvey now thinks it looks like it's probably Kawasaki disease.'

'That's what Harry had.'

'That's right. Let's hope Jamie Bell doesn't end up with the same level of damage.'

Jamie Bell was a very sick little boy.

'Let's have the room dimmed a bit, Kirsty,' was Ian's first suggestion. 'I imagine Jamie's eyes are pretty sore.'

'Shall I fetch a cool face-cloth?' Kirsty pulled the curtains half shut, smiling sympathetically at Jamie's mother who looked younger than herself and very frightened. Jamie was crying but sounded exhausted. His eyes were screwed tightly shut and he lay limply in his mother's arms.

'That's a good idea.' Ian laid a hand on the baby's forehead. 'Find some calamine lotion as well and a clean nappy and maybe a fan. It doesn't look like Jamie's fever is down much yet.'

'He's been like this for more than a week,' his mother said worriedly. 'The GP started him on antibiotics but it didn't help. Then he got this awful rash and they thought it was measles. He seemed to be coming right since we came into hospital but this morning the fever came back. Now they're saying it's something else.' She shook her head miserably and the tears started to roll down her cheeks. 'I've never even heard of what Dr Harvey thought it was. It sounded like the name of a motorcycle.'

'Kawasaki disease.' Ian smiled. 'Why don't you go and have a cup of tea and rest for a bit, Judy? Kirsty and I will look after Jamie and then I'll come and explain it all to you properly.'

'Would you like to have a shower?' Kirsty offered. Judy Bell looked as exhausted as her small son. 'I'll get one of the other nurses to find you a towel and show you where the bathroom is. You might feel a lot brighter after that.'

'I'd love one, but I should stay with Jamie.'

Kirsty held out her arms. 'Don't worry, Judy. Ian

and I love babies. We'll take very good care of him. You need to look after yourself so you can stay well enough to help look after Jamie. Have you had any breakfast?'

'No. I haven't been hungry since we came in.'

Kirsty called one of the student nurses and instructed her to look after Judy. Then she carried the sick baby back into his room and laid him gently on the cot. 'I'll get these pyjamas off,' she told Ian. 'He's way too hot and it smells like he's overdue for a change.'

'He's had diarrhoea for several days. The IV line he had in for fluids tissued just before they brought him over. We'll need to replace that.' Ian was feeling Jamie's neck as Kirsty finished undressing him. 'Cervical lymph nodes are well up.'

'His knees look swollen. And his ankles.' Kirsty rolled up and removed the offending nappy. 'And look at this rash! No wonder they thought it was measles.'

'The swelling and redness of extremities and a rash are two of the first signs of Kawasaki disease,' Ian commented. 'So's this—' Jamie protested more vigorously as Ian checked his eyes. 'Inflamed mucous membranes of the eyes without any discharge.'

Kirsty noted the cracked lips and reached for some petroleum jelly from the trolley as Ian ran his hands down Jamie's arms. The baby cried out miserably as the registrar felt his elbows and then the sound subsided into fretful whimpers as Ian lifted a small hand.

'Look at this, Kirsty. The skin's just starting to peel on his fingers and palms.' Ian unfolded his stethoscope. 'Can you get a temperature while I listen to his chest?'

'It's thirty-nine point seven.' Kirsty reported a minute later. She checked the chart which had come clipped to the end of Jamie's cot. 'It's up again on yesterday. In fact, it went down to normal for a while.'

Ian looked thoughtful. He was still listening to Jamie's chest. The baby made a feeble effort to push the disc of the stethoscope away. Kirsty caught his hand and began to play gently with his fingers, making soothing sounds that were almost a song.

'We're going to need a twelve lead ECG, chest X-ray and echo.' Ian draped his stethoscope back around his neck and stepped over to where Kirsty was now filling a basin with water from the sink. 'He's got first-degree heart block and muffled heart sounds. He may have a pericardial effusion. Recurrence of fever after an afebrile period is a risk factor for development of aneurysms. So's a fever lasting more than sixteen days.' Ian sighed. 'At least he's out of the worst age group, but he's the wrong sex and colour. Caucasian males younger than twelve months are at highest risk.'

'Harry was two when he had it,' Kirsty reminded Ian. 'And then he had a heart attack when he was three.'

'Some cardiovascular changes will resolve. Probably fifty per cent within eighteen months after onset. You can get sudden death from a massive MI anywhere from the third or fourth week after onset. At least we've diagnosed young Jamie here early. We'll be able to treat him and keep a close eye on what's happening to his heart.'

'What's the treatment?' Kirsty wrung out the face-cloth in the bowl of tepid water and began to sponge Jamie down.

'We'll get another IV line in to combat dehydration. We'll start high doses of aspirin—both to get the fever down and deal with the inflamed joints. We'll keep it up during the recovery phase as well to prevent platelet aggregation. Have you got a splint handy? We'd better get this IV line in place.'

Kirsty held Jamie, leaning over the small body to restrain him, one of her hands keeping his arm straight for Ian to work on. She kept close eye contact with the baby and talked constantly to try and distract him.

'We'll find you a lovely ice-block soon,' she told him. 'A lemonade one. And maybe we'll have a nice cool bath. Mummy's having a wash right now. She'll be back very soon.' Kirsty's soothing failed to prevent the outraged wail as the needle penetrated Jamie's arm. Kirsty gritted her teeth and held on until Ian had taped the needle down and then fastened the Velcro straps to hold the splint in place for added protection. Then she picked Jamie up and cuddled him.

'Hold still for a minute.' Ian was gathering some vacutubes. 'We'll get some blood off and then hook up the fluids.'

'Is aspirin the only drug treatment?' Kirsty rocked Jamie gently as Ian waited for each tube to fill.

'No. We'll probably give him IV gamma globulin as well. A single large dose infusion and then a smaller dose for the next five days in combination with the aspirin. I'll check with Charles but it's been shown to be much more effective in preventing coronary artery abnormalities than aspirin by itself. Apart from that, it's basically observation and support nursing. Which you will manage very well.' Ian smiled. Jamie now lay sound asleep in Kirsty's arms. 'I've got a journal article on Kawasaki disease. I got it out of the library when I was reading up on Harry. You might like to borrow it.'

'That would be great,' Kirsty said eagerly. 'I'll drop

in and collect it tonight. I'm off tomorrow so I'll have plenty of time to read it.'

'I'll go and track Charles down now and then explain everything to Judy. It will be good if you do read up a bit as I imagine she'll have a few questions for you over the next few days.'

The remainder of the day passed swiftly. Kirsty was kept very busy looking after Jamie amongst her other patients. Between accompanying her new arrival for an echocardiogram and a chest X-ray, she read several chapters of *The Curse Of The Mummy's Tomb* to Harry. Scheduled for surgery the next day, Harry needed plenty of distraction. Kirsty wasn't sure that the young heroes of the story being pursued by long-dead Eygptian mummies, threatened with boiling tar-pits and being shut into rotting coffins was the best material to distract a young boy about to undergo major cardiac surgery, but Harry was rapt.

'They'll suffocate in that coffin if they can't get out,' he whispered. 'Don't stop reading, Kirsty!'

Kirsty had to stop as Paolo and James Fenwick came to pay a pre-operative visit to their patient. While James showed a polite, if nonplussed, interest in Harry's choice of literature, Paolo manoeuvred Kirsty a little further from the bedside.

'I look forward to Saturday night,' he murmured.

'Me, too,' Kirsty responded with admirable under-statement.

'Do you need a dress?' Paolo took another step back and Kirsty followed his example. 'I have accounts at several high-street stores. I would be delighted to have you choose something especially elegant.'

'No!' Kirsty's eyes widened. She couldn't accept a gift like that. At least, not yet. 'Thanks anyway, Paolo.

I'm sure I've got something suitable.' That was her day off gone, she thought with dismay. She owned nothing that could come anywhere near 'especially elegant'.

'And I'm sure you will look very beautiful.' Paolo gave no indication that his conversation had been anything other than professional as he turned back to the consultant. Kirsty stared after them as they left. She would look very beautiful if it killed her. She would find not only a dress, but some high-heeled shoes to match. And she would find a hairdresser and make an appointment for Saturday morning. With high heels and her hair up surely she couldn't fail to achieve 'elegant'.

'Come *on*, Kirsty. They're suffocating!'

Kirsty tapped on the door of Ian's room at eight o'clock that night.

'Come in,' he invited warmly. 'Did you want that article on Kawasaki disease?'

'Aye, thanks.' Kirsty stood in the centre of the small bedsitting room that was a clone of her own at the other end of the hallway. She had been several times before to share a coffee or listen to music but she seemed ill at ease now. Ian began to sort through a stack of medical journals on the floor.

'Sit down,' he suggested. 'It might take me a minute to find it. I think it was in a copy of *The Lancet*.'

'That's OK.' Kirsty didn't sit down. She paced around and then stopped and cleared her throat. 'Could I ask a favour, Ian?'

'Sure.' Ian sat back on his heels. 'What are friends for?'

'Um.' Kirsty chewed her lip. 'I wanted to get you to write a prescription for me.'

'Are you not feeling well?' Ian's face creased with concern and he stood up swiftly. 'What's the matter?'

'Oh, I'm fine.' Kirsty was looking around the room, avoiding Ian's searching gaze. 'I wanted...I needed a prescription for...um...the pill.'

Ian shut his eyes. This was too much. 'You'd better go and see your GP,' he said heavily.

'I haven't got one.'

'Well, I can't dish out prescriptions for contraceptives.'

'Please, Ian. I need to get started straight away.'

'Even if you started tonight, it wouldn't be effective by Saturday,' Ian snapped. 'There are other methods, you know.' He glared at Kirsty. 'What do you usually use?'

'Nothing.'

'What?' Ian barked. 'Are you crazy?'

'No. Don't shout at me, Ian.' Kirsty looked on the brink of tears. 'I've never needed to use anything. I've never...' Her voice trailed away leaving a stunned silence.

Ian snapped his sagging jaw shut. He felt his anger evaporate completely. 'You mean you've never...' He bit back the beginnings of a smile. 'You mean you're a...a—'

Kirsty clapped her hand over his mouth. 'Don't *say* it! It's embarrassing!' Her cheeks were even redder than her hair. She dropped her hand. 'I've never even *told* anybody.'

'You've told me.' For some reason Ian felt ridiculously pleased. 'It's not embarrassing. I think it's rather special. But, Kirsty—' Ian's pleasure was replaced by dismay '—are you sure you want Paolo to be the one to...I mean, to be the first?'

'Of course I'm sure. Why wouldn't I be?'

'Because it's important. If you've waited this long you must want it to be more than just…sex.' Ian suppressed a wild ray of hope. 'To be really special you have to be in love with someone.'

'Oh, I am.' Kirsty smiled shyly. 'I'm in love with Paolo.'

'Is he in love with you?'

'I don't know.' Kirsty's eyes clouded but then brightened again. 'I wasn't planning to seduce him on the first date, you know, Ian.'

The idea of Kirsty McTavish seducing anyone would have been very humorous if it didn't hurt so much. 'I'm delighted to hear it.'

'I'll leave that up to him,' Kirsty added mischievously. 'I imagine he's much better at it than I'd be.'

'I imagine you're right.' Ian turned back to the journals and extracted the one he'd been searching for. 'Here, take this. I'll see what I can do about arranging a prescription. Just…don't rush into anything, OK? You're worth much more than a one-night stand.'

'Thanks, Ian.' Kirsty looked very solemn. 'And you're right. I'll wait until I'm quite sure he feels the same way about me. It's got to be perfect and I *have* waited a long time.' She smiled hopefully. 'Do you think it'll take much longer?'

Ian shook his head in a mix of amusement and defeat. 'No, Kirsty. I'm sure it won't take very long at all.'

'In spite of my red hair?'

'Go away, Kirsty. I've got work to do.' Ian shut the door firmly behind her but he didn't go back to the books opened on his desk.

Kirsty McTavish was even more innocent than he'd suspected. She was in love for the first time in her life. She was also in love with the wrong man. And there wasn't a damned thing Ian could do about it.

Chapter Three

KIRSTY MCTAVISH had wings on her feet.

It didn't matter that she was flat out coping with the occupants of both the two-bed rooms that were her responsibility for the day. She braided nine-year-old Beth's hair with dexterous rapidity and handed the girl her toothbrush.

'Go down to the bathroom and make every tooth shine,' she instructed. 'Then I'll put another sticker on your chart.'

It was time for Harry's deep-breathing exercises. Five days post-surgery now, Harry had been back from the intensive care unit for two days and was doing very well. The monitoring lines had been removed and he was down to a single IV line in his arm. The metal pole on the mobile IV frame was useful for support as Harry's activity levels increased. His chest incision was healing beautifully and the consultants were very satisfied with his progress. Kirsty took out the surgical glove and felt-tip pen she had ready in her apron pocket. She drew a shape on the glove.

'This is the Blob that ate everyone,' she told Harry. 'But you have to blow up the glove really big to see what he looks like.'

It was a painful effort for Harry to take deep breaths and blow against the resistance the glove provided, but it was a great exercise and he attended to it with deep concentration. Kirsty stood and watched, a large smile curving her lips.

She had never felt so happy. It was enough to make her feel sorry for anybody whose life was not charged with the electricity of high romance. The tingle of anticipation was with her constantly. It carried her through all the mundane tasks of her job, it added to the sheer enjoyment of working with children and it made her feel curiously responsible for Ian Fraser's apparent depression.

'Good boy, Harry. Look at him!' Kirsty stretched the wrist of the glove and deftly knotted it. A gruesome, bloated monster with fingers sticking out of his head was baring sharp fangs at them. Harry grinned.

'Blobs don't have teeth.'

'Some of them do,' Kirsty said firmly. 'Now, let me have a wee look at your chest.' The plastic skin over the incision site was clear. The tissue beneath looked clean and pink. 'You'll be getting those stitches out pretty soon.'

'Good. They're itchy.'

Kirsty wrapped a blood-pressure cuff around Harry's skinny upper arm. 'Is the schoolteacher coming to see you this morning?'

'No.' Harry made a face. 'I have to go to the school room.'

'Do you want to try and walk that far or shall I fetch a wheelchair for you?'

'I'll walk.'

'Good for you. I'll come with you.' Kirsty quickly took Harry's temperature and pulse and recorded the measurements. Then she took a slow walk with her young patient towards the room set aside for school-aged children who were well enough to attend for an hour or two each day. They passed Beth, coming back from the bathroom. She hooked her fingers into her lips and exposed her teeth with alarming enthusiasm. Kirsty put up a hand to shade her eyes.

'I'm dazzled, Beth. I'll come and find you a sticker as soon as I've taken Harry to school. You've got an X-ray first so you'll have to have your lessons a bit late today.'

Beth was hugging herself. Kirsty wasn't sure if the pleasure came from the promise of a sticker or the delay in schoolwork. Probably only the sticker. Beth enjoyed everything, including the patient attention of Mrs Black, the schoolteacher. Mildly affected by Down's syndrome, Beth hadn't been as lucky in the severity to which her heart had been affected by the condition. An episode of heart failure had seen her admitted over the weekend for reassessment and adjustment in her medications. She was almost ready for discharge again now.

Harry and Kirsty also passed Ian on their slow walk. He smiled at Harry.

'You're a champion, kid.'

Harry glowed at the praise and Kirsty smiled her thanks for the encouragement but Ian only nodded, gathered up another set of case notes from the trolley and turned away into one of the single rooms. Kirsty and Harry moved on.

Ian's withdrawal was the only bleak aspect to a life that was falling into place with what could have seemed worrying perfection, except that Kirsty was convinced that this was the way it was meant to be. Paolo felt the same way she did. He had said so— amongst the many whispered endearments in the back of the chauffeur-driven limouisine on Saturday night. Goodness knew what the Italian phrases he had added meant but if his hands and lips had conveyed their meaning it was no wonder he hadn't translated for her verbally. Kirsty had thought she would die from happiness the first moment his lips had touched hers. After the silken thrust of his tongue against hers and the brush of his hand against her breast—inside her dress—Kirsty had changed her mind. She would die of frustration instead.

Mrs Black welcomed Harry. Two other children were already seated at a large table, covered with books, paper, crayons, play dough and puzzles. A third child was writing on a small blackboard.

'Let's find you a comfortable chair, Harry. I've got some great maths puzzles for you today. Did you bring that book you were telling me about?'

Harry nodded. Kirsty handed over the battered paperback. Mrs Black didn't even blink.

'Ah, *The Scarecrow Walks At Midnight*. I'll look forward to hearing you read to me, Harry.'

Kirsty hastened back from the school room. She needed to find someone to accompany Beth to X-ray and the bath for Jamie Bell should be ready by now. Jamie's fever had finally receded but the rash and peeling skin had left him itchy and miserable. Kirsty was going to try and give him a long soak in a soothing bath. It was too early to be sure but Jamie was not showing any signs of serious cardiac involvement from the Kawasaki disease yet.

Kirsty's thoughts slid away from her duties with an alacrity she was becoming accustomed to. She only indulged at moments such as this when it made no difference to her performance. It was easy to switch them off, but the pleasure of allowing their brief but frequent appearances was too great to stifle.

Why had Paolo instructed the chauffeur to take them

back to Lizzie's after the evening at Glyndebourne? Never mind that it was only a first date and Kirsty had done nothing about protection for herself. She had been ready—and more than willing. But Paolo had been gently amused by her disappointment. He had promised another night—a more intimate occasion—at his own home. When it was to be hadn't been finalised. Where it was to be sounded perfect and what was going to happen was just as predetermined as the address. The excited anticipation was enough to make Kirsty very nervous. She had never done anything like this before. Would she be able to perform to an acceptable standard?

Kirsty checked the temperature of the bath and added a good measure of Pinetarsol which turned the water green. Then she moved to the supply room to collect towels and the other items she needed. She was still aware of the butterflies in her stomach at the thought of her next date with Paolo.

'Relax,' she told herself firmly. 'You managed elegant, didn't you?'

The little black dress, the high heels, the swept-up hairdo. Paolo hadn't minded that the enormously fat lady singing the lead part in the opera had sent Kirsty into fits of stifled giggles. He hadn't minded that she had had no idea which fork to use first at dinner and that she had turned her ankle on those awful heels and he'd had to catch her to prevent a nasty fall. In fact, that had started it. Once his hands had been on her body they'd never seemed to leave. It had been Paolo's suggestion that they skipped the second half of the opera after the intermission for dinner. They had sneaked out like truant schoolchildren and explored the lawns and gardens instead, until it had been too dark and getting cold. Then they had summoned the car and snuggled up for the long, but not long enough, drive back into the city.

Perhaps it didn't matter that her friendship with Ian was suffering. Kirsty collected Jamie and they both waved Judy off. Jamie's mother was grateful to get home for a few hours each day to keep up her housework, shopping and care of the rest of her family. Kirsty showed Jamie the green bath and took the soft mittens off his hands, necessary at present to stop further skin damage from scratching but annoying to the toddler who found it difficult to play with his fingers restricted.

'I've got something for you to play with. Look!' Kirsty filled a plastic syringe, minus the needle, with green bath water. Then she injected it rapidly onto the small boy's chest. Jamie shrieked with delight and reached for the syringe. Despite having remembered to don her large plastic apron, Kirsty was soon very damp but as amused by the session as Jamie was. The pleasure wore off a little as she gently patted Jamie dry and anointed the worst areas of skin with a calamine-based lotion.

Of course it mattered that her friendship with Ian was suffering. They had hit it off with each other the very first day Kirsty had started at Lizzie's. She had been touched the first time she'd seen him—his tall, lean figure being followed around the ward by several youngsters like a medical Pied Piper. The children loved him and Kirsty was as intrigued as they were about the contents of the pockets on his white coat. There were always jellybeans, of course, but it was the unexpected that enthralled Ian's devotees. Like the furry black plastic spider with the tube and soft bulb on the end. When Ian squeezed the bulb the spider squeaked and jumped across a lucky patient's bed. Then there was the set of wind-up false teeth with legs that chattered and jumped on a hard surface such as a bedside table—guaranteed to bring a smile to even the most uncooperative small person. Best of all were the magic tricks. The bag with the disappearing egg and the coloured balls that could somehow vanish up the sleeves of the white coat and appear from behind a child's ears or out of a pyjama pocket.

Kirsty put Jamie's mittens back on and took him down to the playroom. He would be well supervised while she attended to cleaning up and catching up with the paperwork her morning's duties had generated so far. She was also due for a coffee break. Kirsty used several towels to mop up the faintly green puddles on the tiled floor of the bathroom.

Ian's furry spider hadn't been seen for days and Kirsty knew the teeth were lying, broken, in the top drawer of Jane Armstrong's desk. Ian was still just as gentle with the children, just as meticulous in his care, but the laughter had gone. Kirsty was determined to cheer him up. Maybe seeing her relationship with Paolo had made him aware of what was missing in his own life. He deserved the excitement of passion as much as she did.

Ian was the *nicest* person Kirsty had ever met. He had made her feel welcome and they had enjoyed each other's company so much that Kirsty had not attempted to strike up more than casual friendships with the other nurses. Maybe she should try and find someone for Ian. Kirsty sighed, just a little. It was hard to imagine Ian being swept into the throes of passion. He was too kind, too much fun to be around. Somehow, red hair, magic tricks and laughter didn't equate with serious romance. A steamy session in the back of a limousine or a sophisticated dinner with far too much cutlery was alien enough to seem ridiculous in conjunction with Ian Fraser. But then, his quiet preoccupation was also alien. It was time Kirsty nudged him out of it.

Finding that Beth had returned from X-ray gave Kirsty her opportunity. Beth adored Ian and she was easily one of his favourite patients.

'Before you go and see Mrs Black,' Kirsty suggested thoughtfully, 'how would you like to help me play a wee trick on Dr Ian?'

Minutes later, Kirsty found Ian in the central office, sorting through the new batch of lab results.

'Ian, can you spare a moment? I'm having a problem getting Beth to cooperate. She wants to talk to you.'

'Can it wait, Kirsty? Charles Bruce will be here in a minute. We're about to start our major ward round.'

'Beth's due for her discharge review, isn't she?'

'Yes, why?'

'I expect you'll want her available for examination. She's under her covers and refusing to come out for anyone except you.'

'That doesn't sound like Beth.' Ian frowned but abandoned the sheaf of lab results to follow Kirsty.

The room Beth shared with Harry appeared deserted. Harry was still in the school room, his bed neatly made up. Beth's bed was distorted by the silent mound under the covers.

'What's all this about, Beth?' Ian stood at the foot of the bed. 'Don't you want to go home?'

His query was greeted by silence. Kirsty looked worried.

'Please come out, Beth, darling. Dr Bruce is coming

to see you and you'll be getting way too hot under there.'

Ian fished in his pocket and Kirsty hid her smile when the furry spider emerged. He placed it on the bed near the edge of the immobile mound.

'Spider's coming to get you, Beth. Watch out!'

The spider bounced and squeaked but gained no response. Ian was just reaching his usual level of enthusiasm when Charles Bruce and Jane Armstrong entered the room. Kirsty's eyes widened.

'Do you think we could make a start on this round, Ian?' Charles Bruce asked mildly. 'We do have an outpatient clinic straight after this.'

'Of course, sorry.' Ian reeled in the spider, wrapping the tube hurriedly around his hand. 'I was just trying to persuade our patient here to come out and see us. She's not too keen this morning.'

Jane Armstrong was eyeing Kirsty thoughtfully. She stepped forward and flicked the bedclothes back. Ian's horrified gaze took in the carefully moulded pile of pillows at the same time as the shrill giggling erupted from under the bed. Kirsty bit her lip. It had only been the promise of two extra stickers that had provided enough of an incentive for Beth to control her delight in the prank and stay silent. Now, she couldn't stop laughing. Kirsty was worried that Beth might wet her pants as her amusement bordered on mild hysteria. Still, it was contagious and Kirsty had to smother her own giggles as she fluffed up the pillows and replaced them at the head of the bed. Ian glared at her as he followed the consultant and charge nurse from the room.

'I'll get you for that, Kirsty McTavish. Your card is marked.'

But the blush had faded and Ian was grinning. Kirsty was well satisfied. She would just make sure she was ready for any retaliation.

The bunch of white roses that arrived for Kirsty on the ward that day only added to the excitement life was offering. The message was handwritten in Italian and everybody knew who they were from. Jane Armstrong's gaze was even more thoughtful than usual as she handed them over to Kirsty.

'Seems like you have an admirer,' was her only comment.

A fluffy white teddy bear with a pink bow arrived for Kirsty the next day. Red roses with a dinner invitation came a day later, shortly before Jade Reynolds was readmitted to the ward.

'You'll wear the words off that card if you don't stop reading it,' Ian said dryly. 'If you can tear yourself away from the flower arranging I'd like you to get a room ready for Jade Reynolds.'

'Oh, is she coming back in?' Kirsty slipped the card into her pocket. 'What's happened?'

'Her GP's sending her in. She's running a fever. Heart-rate's up to one fifty, respiration rate of twenty-nine and her BP's eighty over fifty. Puffy eyes which may indicate fluid retention and some chest crackles. Could be early pneumonia.'

'Oh, poor wee thing.'

'It's a common problem. Pneumonia's often a presenting symptom for heart failure cases. Get a little bit of failure and soggy lungs and it's a good breeding ground for bugs. Her mother's coming in with her. Jane said Room Two is free at the moment.'

'I'll look after it,' Kirsty assured Ian. She turned to the office computer, trying to ignore the vase of red roses she had been arranging for everyone to enjoy. She flicked the computer program onto the welcome banner it could produce and typed 'Jade' into the name space. Stuck on the wall behind the bed, the print-out was a small but effective way of making a child and family feel less lost on admission. Kirsty also searched out 'Mr Red', the puppet with the wobbly eyes. With the puppet's assistance, Kirsty had managed to elicit the delightful smiles of the small girl on many occasions on her last admission.

Kirsty was pleased at the distraction an extra patient would provide for the remainder of her shift. Otherwise, the prospect of a dinner at Paolo's house would have had her nervous anticipation escalating into unbearable tension. She was so well distracted, in fact, that she was entirely unprepared for Ian's eventual retaliation for the almost-forgotten practical joke that Beth had assisted with. Kirsty had seen the gruesome plastic vomit before. She had no idea where Ian found these treasures but she knew he had an unending supply. His timing, this time, was unparalleled.

The visit from the principal nursing officer, Mrs Imogen Drew, was not a regular occurrence. When she appeared in Jane Armstrong's company, later that afternoon, for a tour of the ward, Kirsty was instantly on her best behaviour. She had only met Mrs Drew on one occasion, when she had been interviewed for the nursing position. She had wanted to impress the older woman then and was now eager to demonstrate that the faith in her nursing abilities had not been misplaced. So eager that Kirsty failed to notice the objectionable mess on the floor of Room Four until the horrified gaze of Imogen Drew fastened onto it. Kirsty leapt to rectify the situation, reaching out to pick up the soft plastic, horribly realistic item. Mrs Drew's gasp of horror was followed by Jane Armstrong's resigned sigh. Kirsty stuffed the fake vomit into her pocket, apologising profusely for someone's misplaced sense of humour.

She would kill Ian Fraser at the first opportunity. But Kirsty had to admit the retribution had been perfectly timed. Both Mrs Drew and Jane Armstrong had apparently seen the funny side of the situation quite quickly and the children in Room Four had been beside themselves with amusement.

'It wasn't funny, Ian.' Kirsty was finally heading off duty.

'Everybody else thought it was.'

Kirsty snorted. 'It was very immature. What's the next delight? A fake amputated finger?'

'I think I've got one of those somewhere.'

'I'm sure you have.' Kirsty refused to laugh. 'I don't want to see it. I've grown out of practical jokes.'

'Really?' Ian looked disappointed.

'Really,' Kirsty said firmly. 'I've got far more important—and mature—things to consider. I'm going now. I've got to get ready for a very important occasion.' Kirsty's stomach gave a quick flutter as she remembered what the occasion was likely to be. Then she smiled happily at Ian who grinned back after a momentary hesitation.

'In that case, can I have my vomit back, please?'

It was a setting straight from the pages of a popular romance. The two participants were acting out a preliminary scene that Kirsty had not bothered with in her fantasy rehearsals but it was the perfect way to build up the romantic tension.

The dinner was superb. And Kirsty couldn't taste a single mouthful. The courses came and went, served discreetly by Carlos, the silent butler. The background music was soft and classically romantic. The champagne was icy cold and very easy to swallow. Paolo kept topping up the crystal flute and gradually Kirsty felt her nervousness fade, overridden by the excitement of what was to follow—a scene already well rehearsed in fantasy.

The formal dining room of Paolo's house was impressive. They sat at one end of a table that could have seated sixteen people. The light from the candelabra along the length of the polished mahogany was the only illumination in the room. It was reflected by the silver ice bucket holding the second bottle of champagne. It touched only the edges of the expanse of marble flooring that provided an intimate dance floor to one side of the room and it warmed the already burning gaze Kirsty was receiving from the dark eyes of the man seated very close to her.

The conversation was muted—almost an intrusion to the long-held glances. Kirsty's chatter had been suppressed by tension but her responses to Paolo's gentle questions were eager. He wanted to know if she would like to visit Rome. Of course she would. He told her of all the wonderful places he would take her to. Kirsty became lost in the vision of being in Rome with Paolo. It would be perfect. He murmured about wedding plans and Kirsty's brain mistily absorbed the words through a haze of pure happiness. She focused a little more clearly when Paolo's gaze became noticeably more intense.

'Do you mind, Kirsty? Are you still happy to be here with me, *cara*?'

'Oh, yes,' Kirsty breathed. 'I couldn't be happier, Paolo.'

An eyebrow lifted imperceptibly and then the dark eyes hooded slightly. 'I'm not so sure about that.' He rose lazily to his feet. 'Will you dance with me?'

It couldn't really have been called a dance. They stood, swaying slowly on the gently shadowed marble. Paolo's hands held Kirsty confidently, one on her back, the other soon sliding down to cover her hip and draw her close against him. The folds of the soft moss-green dress did nothing to buffer Paolo's obvious desire for her. Kirsty's hands went up to his neck instinctively as she felt the brush of his chest across her breasts. Her eyes were closed and her lips already parted as the dark head bent towards her own. The gasp as she felt her legs swept from under her was lost in the kiss. Kirsty had no idea how Paolo could see where he was carrying her to and she didn't care. It was finally happening and it was far, far more exciting than any fantasy.

The bedroom was also lit by candles. The satin sheets on the four-poster bed were turned back invitingly. Kirsty couldn't have said how Paolo undressed her. Her clothes just seemed to melt away between the kisses and the rain of passionate Italian. Kirsty needed no translation. She knew, for the first time, that she was beautiful. Desirable. About to be shown what passion really meant by someone who really knew what he was doing. Kirsty had had no need to agonise about whether her response would be acceptable. She could only respond as Paolo's touch inspired. She had no choice—and didn't want any.

The candlelight gilded Paolo's olive skin. He was so gorgeous that Kirsty's breath caught and held and she simply stared as she lay on the bed and watched him fluidly discard his own clothing. Then he was leaning over her, his breath ruffling a curl that had fallen over her cheek, his tongue tracing a path towards her lips.

'*Cristo!*' Paolo's face lifted as he mouthed the soft curse. It was only then that Kirsty became aware of the discreet intermittent buzzing.

'What's wrong, Paolo?' Her voice sounded strange. Husky and distant.

'The phone.' Paolo had moved away. 'A call is only put through if it is an unavoidable emergency. I must answer it.'

The intrusion was unwelcome to say the least. Kirsty pulled the satin sheet over herself reluctantly as Paolo's tone became clipped. The magic was crumbling.

'What is the blood pressure now?' Paolo stood beside the bed. Naked. Looking as magnificent as a Renaissance statue and almost as incongruous.

'Any sign of tamponade?' Paolo listened for a minute. 'OK. We'll have to get her back to theatre immediately. I'm on my way.'

His apologies to Kirsty were sincere. She could see that Paolo was as disappointed as she was herself and just as frustrated. She offered to wait but they both knew the magic had been destroyed.

'Carlos will take you home when you are ready, *cara*.' The kiss had been brief. 'There will be another time.'

He was almost dressed again when a thought occurred to Kirsty. 'Who called you in?'

'The call was from Intensive Care. Our case from this afternoon was having rhythm disturbances. She appears to be bleeding post-surgery. We will have to go in again and find the problem.'

'But who made the phone call?' Kirsty persisted.

Paolo shrugged. 'Ian Fraser.'

'How *could* you, Ian?'

The accommodation quarters were close enough to Lizzie's for the doctors to stay when on call and Kirsty had been pacing the kitchen floor waiting to intercept Ian and vent her frustration. She was far too keyed up to consider going to bed even though it was after midnight.

'How could I what?' Ian opened a cupboard to extract a coffee mug.

'Drag Paolo in. He wasn't even on call.'

'It was his patient. It was an emergency.' Ian put the mug down again and eyed Kirsty. 'How do you know I called him in?'

'I was there,' Kirsty snapped.

'Oh...' Ian's expression altered, leaving his face carefully neutral. 'I interrupted something.'

'You could say that.' Kirsty took a deep breath and glared at Ian furiously. 'You interrupted the *perfect* end to a *perfect* evening. The consummation of my engagement, no less. I hope you're pleased with yourself.'

'Engagement?' Coffee was forgotten.

'Paolo asked me to go to Rome.' Kirsty's anger was receding as she remembered the intimate murmurings over dinner. 'He seems to have already organised the wedding for December.' A smile broke through Kirsty's frown and she shook her head. 'Then he asked me if I minded. *Minded!*' Kirsty gave a small twirl and laughed joyously.

'I guess you don't.' Ian's tongue felt oddly thick. 'I'm sorry I spoilt the celebration, Kirsty.'

'I forgive you.' Kirsty leaned back against the

kitchen counter and smiled brilliantly at Ian. 'Only now I can't possibly sleep. It's too hot and I'm too...'

'Frustrated?' Ian offered blandly.

'Exactly.' Kirsty screwed up her nose. 'And it's all your fault, Ian Fraser.'

'Why don't you go for a swim?'

'A swim! Where, in the canal?'

'No, the physio pool. I know the code for the door.'

'At this time of night?'

'It should be nice and quiet. I've swum there at night before.'

'I don't have a swimming costume.'

'You don't need one. It's dark and there won't be anyone around. There's plenty of towels.'

'I don't know where it is.' Kirsty's eyes were sparkling. The unconventional idea had captured her. 'It would be a lot more fun than having some hot milk. Will you show me how to get there?'

'OK.' Ian glanced at his watch. 'In fact, I'll come with you. I'll have to drop back to Intensive Care later but they won't be out of theatre for a while yet and I've got my beeper if anything else crops up.'

The physiotherapy department was deserted. Ian punched in the code for the door lock and eased it shut behind them.

'Come on, the pool's over the other side of the gymnasium.'

'I've never been in here,' Kirsty whispered. 'It's huge!'

'It's where we'll be holding the Halloween Ball. We'll clear out all the equipment and decorate it. It's far enough away from the wards not to disturb anyone. Have you got a ticket yet?'

'No.'

'I'll get you one,' Ian promised. 'I've got friends on the staff association.'

The ghostly shapes of the pieces of equipment they had to circumnavigate with care in the dark made the gymnasium decidedly eerie. The adventure took on a whole new dimension when Kirsty saw the mirror-like surface of the swimming pool. The room was almost as dark as the gymnasium, the only light coming from high windows located on an outside wall, allowing the street lighting to filter in. For the second time that evening Kirsty watched a man discard his clothing.

'Hurry up, Kirsty. I mightn't have too much time.'

Kirsty pulled off her dress. Then she hesitated. Ian wasn't watching. He was already swimming, his smooth breast-stroke sending ripples across the dark surface of the pool.

'Oh, what the hell?' Kirsty muttered. 'It's only Ian, after all.' She dropped her underwear on top of her dress and slipped into the water.

It was deliciously warm. They swam in silence, both aware that their presence might not be acceptable at this time of night even though selected staff had access to the pool after hours. The silence was entirely companionable. There was no need to express their enjoyment verbally. Kirsty revelled in the caress of the warm water on her body. She had never swum naked before. To have done so alone in a dark pool would have been exhilarating but a little scary. With Ian swimming close by it was exhilarating and magical. Kirsty felt totally relaxed, comforted…and safe.

'How did you know the code for the door?' Kirsty asked as she finally reached for the towel Ian had dropped at the side of the steps.

'I went out with one of the physios for a while when I first came here.'

'Ah! So you *do* have a love life. I was beginning to wonder.'

'We were just friends.'

Kirsty wrapped the towel around herself as she came up the steps. 'Like us, you mean?'

Ian was standing at the top of the steps. He didn't move as Kirsty stopped beside him, using a loose corner of her towel to rub her hair.

'No. Not like us.'

Something in his tone made Kirsty's hand slow its movements and then drop to her side. The intense stare she was receiving reminded her of Paolo. In fact, Ian's brown eyes were only a few shades lighter than Paolo's. The swim had completely erased Kirsty's frustration. She could easily forgive Ian's role in interrupting the perfect seduction scene. She could even forgive the plastic vomit. In the wave of warmth that swept through her she could feel the pull of the same magic her evening had begun with.

Was it Ian or herself that moved closer? Who started the kiss? If she closed her eyes Kirsty could imagine that it was Paolo kissing her. The now familiar surge of desire centred low in her abdomen sent tentacles right through her body. But it wasn't Paolo! Kirsty jerked her head back with an effort, her expression changing rapidly into one of extreme dismay. Ian was watching her silently.

'Oh, God! How did that happen?' Kirsty whispered.

'I'm not sure.' Ian was still watching her carefully. 'But I'm not going to apologise.'

'No.' Kirsty scrambled to find her clothes. 'It's me

who should apologise. I'm the one who's just got engaged. I shouldn't have even come here with you, Ian.'

'It's no big deal.' Ian already had his jeans back on. He was buttoning his shirt as his pager sounded. 'I'll have to go and find a phone. Can you find your own way back, Kirsty?'

'Yes.' Kirsty still sounded flustered. 'I'm sorry, Ian.' She met his eyes hesitantly. 'I'd hate anything to spoil our friendship, you know?'

'It was just a kiss.' Ian tried to sound offhand. 'I've forgotten about it already.'

But he hadn't. The memory of the touch of Kirsty's lips and her response was as clear as it had been amazing. And she *had* responded—whether she had wanted to or not.

She *had* wanted to. Kirsty was appalled with herself. Sure, she wanted to experience passion, but she would not have believed herself capable of switching from one man to another in the blink of an eye. She didn't want Ian. Of course she didn't. He was a friend—a very good friend—but he could never be a lover. She had simply confused him with Paolo for an instant. It was the only explanation for the surge of desire she had experienced. It had been purely sexual frustration due to the interruption of the ultimate seduction she had been willingly subjected to only hours ago. One that would, hopefully, be completed as soon as possible.

Only not tonight. Paolo would be watching over his patient in the intensive care unit for some time yet and it was Ian who would be sharing his company. Tomorrow, or rather today, was Saturday and Paolo was unlikely to appear on the ward. On Sunday, it was Kirsty's turn to start a week on night shift. Something had gone temporarily amiss with the perfect plot all of a sudden and it seemed, inexplicably, to revolve around the lanky figure of Ian Fraser.

Ian found Paolo still dressed in his theatre scrub suit, sitting in the ICU office, writing up his report on the surgery. The conversation regarding the status of their shared patient was brief and satisfactory but Ian didn't leave immediately. He pretended interest in a set of case notes lying nearby—a patient he was familiar with. He glanced up as Paolo yawned expansively and paused again in his writing. 'Kirsty was telling me about your visit to Glyndebourne,' he said casually.

'Ah! It was so funny, Ian. Like having to look after a naughty child.'

Ian raised an eyebrow. 'Perhaps she was embarrassed at being socially out of her depth.'

'Not at all.' Paolo laughed. 'She was magnificent! You should have seen her in the little black dress with her hair all piled up.' Paolo sucked in his breath in deep appreciation. '*Fantàstica!* James Fenwick was also at Glyndebourne that night. He kept staring at Kirsty. I think it took some time for him to recognise her.' Paolo sighed. 'She is going to become a very beautiful woman.'

'She already is.' Ian made another show of leafing through the case notes beside him.

'She is still a child,' Paolo stated fondly. 'She needs to experience life. And love.'

'With you?' Ian tried to keep his voice neutral.

'Why not?' Paolo's tone matched Ian's.

'Because…' Ian shook his head and shut the set of case notes. He looked directly at the older registrar. 'Tell me, Paolo—are you engaged?'

Paolo blinked. 'Who told you this?'

'Does it matter?'

Paolo shrugged. 'Of course not. I just didn't think many people knew. Chantelle lives in Paris.'

'Chantelle?' Ian's eyes widened.

'My fiancée. We met a few months ago at the wedding of my first wife.'

Ian was staring at Paolo who seemed to have forgotten his report and was now gazing dreamily off into space.

'Your *first* wife? How many have you had?'

Paolo chuckled. 'Only two, Ian. You make it sound like I am a complete cad.'

'And Chantelle will be number three.'

Paolo nodded. 'She is very beautiful. A model. Very tall, very blonde.'

'And Kirsty?' Ian could feel the stirring of outrage. 'Where does Kirsty fit in?'

'She is also beautiful.' Paolo pursed his lips thoughtfully. 'But not tall and definitely not blonde.'

'She's in love with you,' Ian said accusingly.

'And I am in love with her.' Paolo smiled. 'It will be magnificent—for both of us.' Paolo's glance was amused. 'If you don't manage to interrupt us again, of course.'

'Kirsty is planning to go to Rome.'

'Yes. I will enjoy showing her my city. I will be inviting her to my wedding.'

'I'm not sure she would appreciate the invitation.'

'Why not?' Paolo looked genuinely puzzled. 'She wants to travel. We are friends.'

'I think Kirsty wants to be more than a "friend".' Ian spoke slowly. He was beginning to feel sick. Kirsty obviously didn't have the faintest idea how wrong she was about Paolo. How could she have got such important information so confused? And Paolo seemed to have no inkling about how much she would be hurt by finding out. Even now, when Ian could easily imagine the physical harm he would want to inflict on anybody that hurt Kirsty, it was difficult to resist Paolo's charm. The man adored women and he was generous with his attentions. Perhaps the women he usually chose accepted their eventual fate. But Kirsty wasn't one of them.

Paolo was meeting Ian's accusing stare with a concerned expression. He spoke more seriously than usual with no hint of an accent. 'You think I am insensitive, Ian. I have no intention of hurting Kirsty. I have explained about my future plans, my wedding. She understands.' A smile tugged at the corners of his mouth. 'Kirsty wants to be loved. She wants to know that she can arouse passion in a man. It is a gift I can give. One I hope she would not forget.'

'Oh, she won't forget.' Ian held Paolo's gaze for a long moment before turning away. There really wasn't any way he could prevent the inevitable and perhaps Paolo was right. Kirsty needed to experience what life—and love—had to offer. Otherwise, how would she ever be able to recognise the genuine article? If Ian looked past the anger he felt that Kirsty was going to be hurt he had to confess to relief. Mixed with the relief Ian also acknowledged a spark of hope.

The crash would come. And he would make sure he was there to help pick up the pieces.

Chapter Four

THE crash came with unexpected swiftness.

Ian Fraser was in the communal kitchen for the third floor of the staff quarters when he heard the door slam. He tipped the last dregs of his coffee into the sink and hurriedly rinsed his mug. The sound had come from Kirsty McTavish's end of the corridor. The impact of the disturbance on residents who might well have been sleeping was so insensitive and so far out of character for Kirsty that Ian was alerted to the probability of a major catastrophe.

Leaving the kitchen, Ian passed Josie, another nurse who lived in on the same floor of the residence.

'I wonder who rattled her cage.' Josie grinned. 'Lucky the door didn't fall off its hinges.'

Ian knew exactly who the culprit was likely to be. He tapped on Kirsty's door.

'Go away.' The voice was muffled. Anguished.

Ian tried the handle and found the door unlocked. He shut it quietly behind him, pressing his lips firmly together to suppress a smile. Kirsty was entirely under the covers of her bed and she had dragged the pillow in with her. A strangled sob emerged through the shroud of bed linen. Ian sat down on the space the removal of the pillow had created. He cautiously patted the shaking mound beside him.

'It's only me, Kirsty. Come out and tell me what's wrong.'

'No.'

'Please?' Ian's patting became a soothing stroke. 'I'd like to help. I feel as though this is partly my fault.'

The mound shifted. Kirsty's head emerged, red curls tousled into disarray, heavy smudges of mascara framing huge, agonised blue eyes. She looked rather like a distressed raccoon.

'Why is it your fault?'

'I introduced you to the guy. At least, I'm assuming here that it *is* Paolo who's upset you.'

'*Upset* me!' Kirsty's voice was a squeak. Her ragged indrawn breath was more than half a sob. 'He's *destroyed* me.' Tears welled and rolled down over the freckles.

'Oh, Kirsty,' Ian murmured gently. He held out his arms and Kirsty wriggled closer, burying her face against his shoulder as she sobbed noisily. Ian's hand went to the back of her head, his fingers sliding beneath the curls, his thumb slowly stroking the nape of her neck. He had pictured doing exactly this after his conversation with Paolo only two nights ago. He was surprised to find the anticipation didn't lessen the pain he felt on Kirsty's behalf. He waited for several long minutes until Kirsty calmed down.

'What's he done, exactly?' he asked quietly. For a horrified moment Ian wondered if Kirsty had been physically harmed. If that was the case then no amount of charm could protect Paolo Tonolo from Ian's wrath.

'It's what he's *going* to do,' Kirsty wailed. 'He's going to get *married*!'

Ian nodded wearily. 'I know.'

'No, you don't understand.' Kirsty pushed herself up, her face only inches away from Ian's. 'He's not going to marry *me*! He's getting married to someone else.'

'How did you find out?'

'He *told* me!' Kirsty was outraged. 'I was at his house. We were going to go out for an early dinner but Paolo said we couldn't because he had to go to the airport to collect his *fiancée*!' Her expression changed to one of bemusement. 'He said he thought I already knew—that he'd told me all about the wedding.'

'Had he?'

'Yes…but…' Kirsty's face crumpled again '…I thought he was talking about us.' She stared at Ian incredulously. 'I thought he loved *me*.'

'He does. He told me so himself.'

'Ha!' Kirsty uttered in disgust. 'He doesn't know the meaning of the word.'

'And you do?'

The small toss of her head made Kirsty's curls bounce. 'Of course I do. I love Paolo. I want to be with him—for ever.'

'And Paolo loves you. Adores you,' Ian added calmly. 'He wants to share a passionate relationship with you.'

Kirsty snorted. 'Only when his *fiancée* is unavailable. That's not love.'

'It's a kind of love,' Ian persisted. 'Isn't that what you wanted? Excitement, passion? An irresistible romance?'

'No.' Kirsty's legs unfurled and she sat on the side of the bed. She shook her head violently but the shake became a slow nod as it ended. 'Yes. Of course it is. But there has to be more.'

'Like what?'

'Like commitment.' Kirsty sniffed loudly. 'Like a future. I want *love*, not just sex. No matter how great that might be.'

Ian's heart sank. So it had been great. When had Paolo changed their plans for the evening? Before or after the session in bed?

'I don't think Paolo intended to hurt you.' Why on earth was he defending the guy? 'I think he thought he was simply providing what you wanted.'

'Paolo is a bastard,' Kirsty announced firmly. 'And that's what I told him. I also told him I never wanted to see him again as long as I lived.'

'What did he say to that?'

'I didn't give him a chance to say anything.' Kirsty sighed dramatically. 'I walked out.'

'Perhaps he'll change his mind. About his fiancée.'

'I don't care if he does. I'm giving up on romance. I'm giving up on men. Especially exotic men.'

'Don't give up on me.' Ian smiled. He resisted the urge to try and draw Kirsty back into his arms. Now was definitely not the time to express his own feelings. 'I'm not exotic.'

'No.' Kirsty's smile was forlorn. 'I guess you're safe. I'll just give romance a wide berth.' She pushed herself dejectedly to her feet. 'I have to get ready for work. I'm starting nights tonight.'

'Oh, bad luck,' Ian said sympathetically. Nobody really enjoyed their stint of night duty.

'I'm not bothered,' Kirsty responded flatly. 'My life is over. Why should I care if I don't see any daylight for a week?'

The ward was a different place without Kirsty's presence. To outward appearances it was quite normal. Busy, noisy and cheerful, but Ian Fraser found it significantly lacking. It made him realise just how much he enjoyed the glimpses he had of Kirsty working, the sound of her laughter and the relief from pressure that snatches of conversation or shared jokes could provide. Not that she would be laughing much even if she were present at the moment. The pale face and heavily shadowed eyes that Ian had observed on Monday night couldn't be entirely due to an inability to sleep during daylight hours. Kirsty McTavish was devastated. Paolo Tonolo was also upset.

'I had no idea she felt like that, Ian.' Paolo's hands rose in an eloquent expression of contrition. 'I feel terrible. I have to make things right but she won't talk to me.'

'Don't push it.' Ian handed over the angiography reports he had brought into Paolo's office. 'I think she needs some time to herself.'

'But it was unforgivable. She was so angry when I told her Chantelle was arriving. I thought she understood about my plans for marriage.'

'She did.' Ian shrugged. 'Unfortunately, she somehow got the idea that she was to be the bride.'

'Such a misunderstanding.' Paolo sighed heavily. 'Chantelle and I also had a misunderstanding. It was not a happy time.' He shook his head sadly. 'Women can be difficult to manage sometimes.'

'I wouldn't know,' Ian said bluntly. 'I don't usually try to juggle more than one at a time.'

'But why was Kirsty so upset?' Paolo sounded wistful. 'We hadn't even become lovers.'

Ian was aware of a wave of emotion that he recognised as relief. He could even let go of the knot of resentment he had been harbouring towards his colleague.

'She realised that you are just not able to offer her what she really wants, Paolo. That's what upset her.'

'But why? I can offer her anything. Everything!'

'Commitment?' Ian suggested dryly. 'Fidelity? True love?'

'True love—absolutely! But fidelity?' Paolo whistled silently. 'To stay with only one woman for ever? It could never work.'

'Some people like the idea.' Ian was amused by Paolo's overdone expression of dismay. 'People like Kirsty.' And me, he added silently.

'I need a drink,' Paolo declared. 'Will you come to the pub with me, Ian?'

'I'm on call,' Ian responded. 'And I'd better get back to the ward. We've got a few rather sick children at the moment.'

One of them was Jade Reynolds. She was not responding well to antibiotics. Ian noted her increased fluid retention with concern. The small girl's weight had increased significantly over the last two days and her fever had not decreased despite the change of antibiotics after the organism causing the pneumonia had been identified by culture.

The heart failure was proving very difficult to manage due to the added stress of infection. Ian spent nearly an hour carefully examining the girl and going over the most recent test results later that evening. He was still on the ward, filing some of Jade's results in her case notes, when Kirsty appeared on duty after the staff change-over meeting at eleven-thirty p.m.

Ian stared in surprise. Kirsty had done something weird with her hair. The riot of curls had somehow been scraped back to lie flat against her head and the confined length had been tortured into some sort of knot at the back.

'You look…different,' Ian said worriedly. 'Are you OK, Kirsty?'

'I'm fine, thanks, Ian. I've got Jade top on my list for tonight. I just came to have a look at her notes. I hear she's not doing so well.' Kirsty's blue eyes darkened with distress. Her genuine affection for the shy blonde four-year-old was well known and reciprocated.

'No. Her serum digoxin levels are still all over the place and the electrolyte profile isn't great. I've just charted an oral potassium supplement to see if we can balance things. I'd like a twenty-four-hour urine collection too so I can evaluate the fluid balance more accurately.' Ian was still staring at Kirsty. Why did her face look so different? Her eyes seemed larger and the generous proportions of her mouth seemed to have shrunk. Perhaps it was because it was so unusual not to see Kirsty with at least some hint of a smile on her face. Was it just because of her concern for Jade? 'Are you sure you're OK, Kirsty? You look…' Ian paused, musing.

'Older?' Kirsty suggested. 'Wiser?' Her smile was a sad echo of her normal vivacity. 'I am.' She patted her head briefly. 'This is part of my new, mature image. You were quite right, Ian.'

'I was?'

'It's time I grew up. Time I learned to distinguish between romance and true love. You must have thought I was a complete idiot, full of starry-eyed fantasies like some naïve teenager.'

That was what it was. The stars had definitely gone. Along with the sparkle that had made Kirsty's company so enchanting. 'Don't give them all away,' Ian said quietly. 'I liked the way you were.'

'Too late,' said Kirsty firmly. 'I've grown up. Reality rules.'

Ian smiled. 'Reality can be good, too. And you *can* have romance and true love at the same time.'

'We'll see.' Kirsty sighed. 'I'll certainly look before I leap next time. Nobody's going to sweep me off my feet again. I'm going to go and see Jade.'

'I'll come with you. I want to listen to her chest again. I've put in a request for a repeat echo first thing in the morning. She's got quite a collection of pericardial fluid. We'll probably have to do a pericardiocentesis and drain it. We're having enough trouble controlling her heart failure without further complications from fluid build-up.' Ian glanced over his shoulder at Kirsty as she followed him along the corridor. 'Do you know what signs to watch for that might indicate tamponade?'

Kirsty nodded. A tamponade meant sufficient pressure from fluid around the heart to prevent it functioning adequately. It was potentially a precursor for cardiac shock which could be fatal. 'Increased heart-rate, decrease in blood pressure. Increase in venous pressure, pulsus paradoxus, respiratory distress and chest pain.' Her tone was calm and professionally competent. Ian blinked. She even *sounded* older and wiser.

'Do her observations at least hourly,' Ian suggested. 'If you're at all worried, then beep me.'

The call that brought Ian back to the ward came at almost three a.m. He entered Jade Reynolds' room to find the small girl awake and distressed. She was propped leaning forward on several pillows. Kirsty was sitting beside her, one hand holding an oxygen mask close to the child's face, the other holding Jade close to her body. The red curls were mingled with the wispy blonde hair as Kirsty murmured softly into the girl's ear. The fluffy red puppet lay discarded on the end of the bed. Kirsty glanced up as Ian entered the room, her expression tense.

'I've called in the echo technician on call that you requested. She's bringing the mobile equipment and should be here within half an hour.'

'Where's Barbara?' Ian was surprised that Jade's mother was not present.

'She went home. One of the boys has a stomach bug and was vomiting everywhere. He wanted her to stay with him overnight.'

Ian noted the exaggerated chest movements of the small girl as she breathed. He also noted the distended veins on the side of her neck that indicated a high venous pressure. Jade was trying to cry but couldn't achieve much in the way of volume. Ian listened to her chest only briefly. The heart sounds were muffled to the point of almost total obscurity. He hooked his stethoscope around his neck decisively and pushed the call button beside Jade's bed. A junior nurse appeared immediately.

'Bring in the crash cart from the treatment room, would you, please?'

Kirsty's arm tightened protectively around Jade.

'I'm going to give her a bit of IV Valium,' Ian explained. 'Enough to sedate her. We'll need an angio-cath and a chest drain set-up as well. We can't wait until tomorrow. We're going to have to relieve this fluid build-up stat.' Ian glanced at the IV line. 'Take another blood-pressure reading, would you, please, Kirsty?'

'Seventy over forty,' she reported a minute later. Ian had just snapped off the top of a small glass vial. He inserted a needle and drew the liquid back into the syringe, discarding the vial onto the top of the trolley. 'Increase the flow on the IV,' he ordered. 'We need to ensure adequate right ventricular filling and cardiac output until we can relieve this tamponade.' Ian held the syringe of valium at eye-level, tapping on the barrel of the syringe to release air bubbles. Then he depressed the plunger until a tiny fountain of liquid cleared the tip of the needle. He injected the sedative slowly into the port on the IV line. Within seconds Jade's distress lessened and her eyes fluttered drowsily half shut.

'I'm just going to wake Charles Bruce up,' Ian told Kirsty. 'He may want to come in and do this himself. I'll get someone to contact Jade's family as well.'

Heidi, the echo technician on call, arrived as Ian returned. He helped the diminutive blonde to push the bulky echo machine into place beside Jade's bed. Kirsty positioned herself with Jade lying in her arms, still but flat enough for Heidi to manoeuvre the transducer.

'This doesn't hurt a bit,' Kirsty whispered to Jade. 'It might just tickle your ribs a wee bit.'

'That's good,' Ian commented after several minutes of intent observation of the screen. 'Mark that spot. I'm just going to scrub up.' He caught Kirsty's eye. 'Can you give me a hand? Charles is leaving it up to us.'

Kirsty swapped places with the junior nurse. She scrubbed her hands quickly and edged another trolley in beside the echo machine.

'Swab the area around where we've marked and drape her,' Ian instructed. 'That's right over the largest accumulation of fluid and should give us the best access. Then draw up some local for me.'

Ian felt along Jade's tiny rib and slid the needle in

above it to avoid the nerve structures. Kirsty peeled back the edges of a small packet and presented Ian with the sterile scalpel. He made a tiny nick in the area he had just anaesthetised. Kirsty had the hollow angiocath ready for Ian to grasp. Heidi kept her transducer in position and Ian concentrated intently, watching the screen and advancing the needle slowly until it was inside the pocket of fluid. Kirsty watched as he drained off the initial collection.

'Right. I need a floppy tip guide wire and then we'll have the drainage tube and a three-way tap.'

Kirsty ripped open the packages, careful to expose but not touch the contents as she handed them to Ian. The needle was removed once the guide wire was in position, then the drainage tube was threaded over the wire. When the wire was removed, Kirsty attached the tube to the sealed drainage bottle while Ian sutured the other end of the tube securely.

'I'm putting in a purse string suture first,' he told Kirsty. 'That way, when the tube is removed, we can just tighten it and seal the entry site.'

It was nearly five a.m. before Ian was ready to leave the ward. He signalled to Kirsty, sitting in the office with Jade's mother, Barbara, who was still very upset.

'I should never have gone home.'

'You were needed there as well,' Kirsty reminded her gently. 'Now, how about that cup of tea? Milk and two sugars, isn't it? You won't want to frighten Jade by being so upset when you see her.' Kirsty rose to her feet and met Ian just outside the door.

'How's Jade?'

'Stable, for the moment. I'll have another word with Barbara and then try and grab some sleep. Call me if you need me, otherwise I'll come back in a couple of hours.'

'You'd better get some sleep,' Kirsty advised. 'I go off duty at seven-thirty a.m. You've still got a full day to put in.'

Ian shrugged. 'Comes with the territory.' He rubbed a hand wearily over his forehead. 'I'll be pleased when you've finished nights.'

'Was I that bad an assistant?'

Ian smiled. 'I miss having you around in the day-time. And I miss our running in the park. I'm getting fat and flabby.'

'Yeah, right!' Kirsty smiled, really smiled, seemingly for the first time in days. 'Turn sideways and you still look like a zipper.'

Ian was watching Kirsty's face intently. 'That's better,' he said gently. 'Don't stop smiling, Kirsty.' He began to walk away but then paused. 'You were not a bad assistant, by the way, Nurse McTavish. In fact, when you're behaving yourself you're an extremely good nurse.' He walked another few steps and his soft call broadened Kirsty's smile even further. 'Actually, you're still an extremely good nurse even when you're not behaving yourself.'

Kirsty expected to see a good improvement in Jade's condition by Wednesday night but she was disappointed. By Thursday night the four-year-old girl had been transferred into Intensive Care. Ian was not feeling optimistic. He spoke to Kirsty briefly as she left work on Friday morning.

'We're going to give the antibiotics a chance for another day or so unless there's further deterioration, but it looks like it could need surgical intervention to create a pericardial window for more extensive drainage.'

'What are her chances?'

'Not great. If it goes on to endocarditis and involves the valves we'll be looking at intensive antibiotic therapy for about six weeks. Even without this complication she's already got a damaged heart from the myocarditis. If she survives until adolescence then transplant might be an option.'

'How's Barbara coping?'

'Not very well.'

'I'm not surprised.' Kirsty sighed heavily. 'Jade's the only girl in the family. She's got three older brothers. Barbara told me she'd always desperately wanted a daughter. She said she thought it was too good to be true when Jade was born and that this is like some sort of punishment for wanting something too much.'

'She's depressed—understandably. I'll get up to ICU and visit them shortly. Barbara may need some help to cope with this.'

Kirsty felt as if she could do with some help herself. The night duties were taking a heavy toll on her. She would pull her curtains and crawl into bed at eight a.m., having had a shower but too tired to contemplate a meal. Any sleep she managed was intermittent and unrefreshing. Kirsty was worried about Jade and concerned for Barbara. She could sympathise with Barbara's self-recrimination and depression. Her own was negligible by comparison but still very real. She had set her heart on a passionate romance. Paolo had been too good to be true—and now she was paying for it.

Friday was her last night duty. Kirsty had the weekend off and was to return to morning duties the following week. She was dreading having to encounter Paolo possibly on a daily basis. He had stopped trying to call her after a couple of days. The yellow roses had been left to wilt deliberately in the ward office until Jane Armstrong had rescued them. The card had been shredded, unread.

Kirsty managed only a few short hours of sleep on Saturday morning and was awake again by eleven a.m. Her first thought was to wonder whether Jade Reynolds had survived the night and how Barbara could possibly cope if she hadn't. It certainly put her own emotional tragedy into perspective. Kirsty threw back the covers of her bed impatiently. It was more than time she pulled herself together.

The sight that greeted her in the bathroom mirror made Kirsty wince. A week of interrupted sleep patterns, poor diet and lack of exercise compounded by emotional disturbance had wreaked havoc. Her eyes appeared sunken, ringed by shadows that looked blue against her pale skin. Her cheeks were hollowed and even her curls seemed to be lying flatter than they ever had before, probably due to the restrained style Kirsty had adopted for working hours. She was forced to smile ruefully at her reflection.

'I guess it's one way to lose weight,' she muttered. No wonder Ian had been clucking over her like a mother hen recently. He had even marched her to the staff dining room last night and supervised every mouthful of a three-course dinner despite her protests. He had patiently put up with her arguments and complaints and Kirsty had known her threat of having him wear her dessert had been very immature. Secretly, she had been delighted that someone cared enough to try and bully her into looking after herself. Ian's firm common sense and good humour were a lot more than she deserved. Kirsty had to admit she had felt a lot better after the first decent meal she'd had in almost a week.

A shower and hair wash chased away some of her overwhelming fatigue and fluffed up her curls to normal heights. Make-up took care of the worst discolouration around her eyes and Kirsty added lipstick to give her face a little more colour. She dressed in her favourite faded blue jeans and a soft, cream silk blouse.

The patch of deep blue sky she could see from her window advertised a gorgeous autumn day. Perhaps a walk in Regent's Park and a good dose of UV rays would restore both her colour and her equilibrium. Even mild depression was an alien experience for Kirsty McTavish and she would welcome any assistance in snapping out of it. Kirsty decided she would just make a quick visit to the ICU first and check on Jade's condition.

Jade Reynolds was the centre of a buzz of activity in the intensive care unit. James Fenwick was examining the young patient with several colleagues while both Jade's parents hovered anxiously nearby. Kirsty didn't approach the group. Instead, she had a word with the house officer working at the central desk.

'What's up with Jade?'

'They're going to take her up to theatre. She's reaccumulated a pericardial effusion and the drainage tube has tissued. Mr Fenwick's going to do a thoracotomy and put another drain in.'

'How are her lungs looking?'

'Not bad, but she's still running a temperature.' The house officer moved away quickly as an alarm sounded from the bank of equipment surrounding another small

patient. Kirsty felt she was in the way and moved towards the doors of the unit.

The vending machine in the foyer reminded Kirsty
that she had not bothered with any breakfast again. Ian
would have something to say about that if he knew.
Having inserted a coin, she pushed buttons to dispense
coffee and sugar into the polystyrene cup. Then she
added boiling water. Ian would not have approved of
the black coffee but at least it was something.

Stirring the coffee, Kirsty gazed at two disgruntled
children, sitting slumped onto the waiting area couch.
They looked as though they had been there for some
time and would much rather be somewhere else. The
girl had the laces of a pair of skates knotted together
and the boots were draped over her shoulder. The boy
had a skateboard balanced on his knees. Kirsty gave
them a sympathetic smile but failed to lighten the sul-
len expressions of the children. She turned away to
look out of the window, sipping her coffee. She could
see the treetops in Regent's Park and was suddenly
eager to be well away from Lizzie's. Maybe she would
go for a run this evening. No exercise for a week
wasn't helping the state of her mind or body. Kirsty's
introspection was infiltrated by the sound of an argument in progress behind her.

'But, Dad. You *promised*.'

'It's not *fair*!' A thump suggested the rejection of a
pair of skates or possibly a skateboard being dropped.
Kirsty turned.

'I told you I might get called in for an emergency.
I'm sorry, but there's nothing I can do.'

'So what are we supposed to do?' The girl's voice
was petulant. 'Sit around here for hours waiting for

you? Mrs Benny's gone to visit her sister for the afternoon.'

'You're old enough to look after George.' James Fenwick was looking harassed. 'I'll order a taxi to take you home.'

'I don't want Sarah looking after me.' The younger boy's lip protruded belligerently. 'I want to go skateboarding. You *promised*!'

'I've said I'm sorry.' James Fenwick was looking over the shoulder of his son, watching as Jade's bed was transferred into one of the lifts. 'Look, I've got to go.'

Kirsty had approached the tense trio quietly. 'Perhaps I could be of some help, Mr Fenwick?' She smiled at the children who glared back at her, as though convinced all adults were out to make their lives as miserable as possible. She glanced at the surgeon. 'Are these your children?'

'Yes.' James Fenwick smoothed a hand over his hair. 'Sarah's fourteen and George is ten. I had promised to take them skating in Regent's Park this afternoon but unfortunately there's been an emergency. Paolo could have dealt with it but his grandmother is ill yet again and he took off back to Rome this morning.'

Kirsty tried to ignore the pang the mention of Paolo's name gave her. 'Cool skates,' she told Sarah. 'I used to go roller-blading.'

'These aren't roller blades—they're roller balls. They're new and I haven't even had a chance to try them out yet.' The girl shot her father an accusing glance.

'I was just planning on a walk in the park myself,' Kirsty told them. 'Maybe we could go together.'

James Fenwick looked at Kirsty with new interest.

'I'm afraid I couldn't possibly impose on you…Kirsty, isn't it?'

'Yes. Kirsty McTavish. I'm a nurse up on Cardiology.'

'Of course. How could I forget? You came and observed during Amy Pennock's surgery.'

'And it wouldn't be an imposition,' Kirsty added eagerly. 'As I said, I'm going to the park anyway. I could use some company.' Kirsty grinned at Sarah. 'In fact, I wouldn't mind a go on those flash-looking skates, myself.'

'How would that suit you, children?' James Fenwick was already looking towards the lifts. 'I should be well finished by the time you get back and then we could go and have some dinner together. You can choose the restaurant.'

'McDonald's,' both children stated with alacrity.

James Fenwick shuddered. 'We'll see. Have fun.' He smiled warmly at Kirsty. 'Thank you very much, Miss McTavish.'

'Kirsty,' she corrected. She waited until the surgeon had reached the door of the lift, then she eyed the children who were still regarding her with some suspicion. 'I'd vote for McDonald's, too,' she informed them. 'Now, shall we go and terrorise a few little old ladies in Regent's Park?'

The afternoon was the perfect antidote for a week of misery. Kirsty and Sarah shared the same shoe size and the ice was well and truly broken when Kirsty fell onto her bottom at her first attempt to skate and let loose with some very colourful oaths. George tried to teach her to turn his skateboard but Kirsty gave up in favour of watching the boy's expertise. Genuinely impressed, Kirsty won George over completely.

'It's nothing,' he said modestly. 'You could probably get the hang of it eventually, too.'

'I think I'm getting a bit old,' Kirsty decided.

'How old *are* you?' Sarah demanded.

'Twenty-four,' Kirsty replied. Going on sixty, she added to herself. But her new efforts at a mature outlook on life were difficult to maintain in the company of two children who were beginning to relax and enjoy themselves. Kirsty wondered how much time they spent with their father. Did they only see him on weekends due to a separation of their parents, perhaps? She couldn't imagine James Fenwick out skating with his offspring. Kirsty jogged along behind the children, feeling steadily hotter.

'Let's go and find an ice cream,' she called. They slowed rapidly to let Kirsty catch up. She grinned at Sarah. 'And then I'd like another go on those skates.'

It was surprising how fast the afternoon had gone. Kirsty delivered Sarah and George back to Lizzie's and paged James Fenwick from the main reception desk. The surgeon appeared quickly but Kirsty was surprised when he veered into the flower and fruit shop, Dunwoody. She was even more surprised when he emerged again carrying a small bouquet of flowers wrapped in Cellophane.

'By way of thanks,' he explained.

'You're welcome.' Kirsty smiled as she accepted the bouquet. Thank goodness they weren't roses! 'We had fun, didn't we, guys?'

Both children nodded though Kirsty noticed the subduing effect the presence of their father had made.

'Unfortunately, I'm a bit out of practice on wheels,'

Kirsty said brightly. 'I may have trouble sitting down tomorrow.'

George grinned. 'You should have heard Kirsty when she fell over, Dad.'

'Indeed?' James Fenwick gave George a searching gaze which was transferred to his daughter as Sarah gave her brother a warning poke in the ribs. She spoke quickly in a transparent attempt to change the subject.

'Is Kirsty going to come to McDonald's with us, Dad?'

'I…ah…' James Fenwick looked embarrassed.

'I can't, I'm sorry,' Kirsty apologised swiftly. 'Maybe another time.'

'Will you come skating with us again?'

'I'd love to,' Kirsty responded warmly. 'I'm not often off duty at weekends, though.'

'We could go after school,' George suggested. 'Mrs Benny doesn't like going to the park.'

'Oh?' Kirsty was beginning to feel uncomfortable.

'Mrs Benny is our housekeeper,' James Fenwick explained.

'Mum died,' George added. 'When I was seven.'

Kirsty felt even more uncomfortable. She was a junior staff member and James Fenwick was one of the top consultants at Lizzie's. She had heard it rumoured that a knighthood was a foregone conclusion in the near future. She doubted that he would want her privy to details of his private life. But James Fenwick appeared quite relaxed.

'You seem to have made a hit with my children, Kirsty. Perhaps we *could* arrange another outing some time when you're free.'

Kirsty nodded nervously but then grinned. 'Maybe

I'll invest in a pair of my own skates and get some practice in. I'd really enjoy seeing Sarah and George again, Mr Fenwick.'

'Call me James,' he invited. 'I'll be in touch, Kirsty.'

Chapter Five

'YOU look like an electrocuted fish!'

'Gee, thanks.' Kirsty closed her wide-open mouth and smiled sweetly at Ian. 'You're looking pretty good yourself.'

'What's in the box? Another attempt to persuade you to forgive Paolo?'

Kirsty's chin went up sharply. 'I wouldn't have opened it if it was.'

'Did you hear that his grandmother really *was* sick, this time? She died yesterday. Paolo will be away all week.'

'Good.' Kirsty looked inappropriately delighted.

Ian's eyebrows shot up. 'She was only eighty-five. She might have been a very nice old lady.'

'I didn't mean good that she died,' Kirsty said hurriedly. 'I'm just glad Paolo's away. I was planning to hide in the sluice room whenever he appeared on the ward.'

'A very mature way to deal with it.' Ian nodded. 'You have my approval. So, what's in the box?'

'Would you believe a pair of roller blades?'

'I'll believe anything where you're concerned, Kirsty McTavish. Are you planning to increase your efficiency by attending to your duties on wheels?'

Kirsty grinned. 'Sounds fun but I doubt that Jane would approve. I'll stick to Regent's Park.'

Ian was relieved to see Kirsty looking so much more cheerful. Being on duty over the weekend, he hadn't seen her and she had clearly pulled herself together admirably. Kirsty was bouncing back. Maybe now was a good time to step into the gap Paolo had left.

'I'll come with you, if you like. Where did you get the skates?'

'I didn't. They're a gift from James.'

'James?' Ian swallowed with some difficulty. Surely forty-eight hours hadn't been leaving it too long to offer to take up the slack in Kirsty McTavish's romantic saga?

'Mmm.' Kirsty was shaking her head in bemusement. 'James Fenwick.'

'Mr Fenwick?' Ian remembered the surgeon's tolerant amusement at meeting Kirsty for the first time having been treated to a sample of her singing. An image of the ultimately well-groomed consultant in his three-piece pinstriped suit sprang to mind. So did Paolo's comment that James Fenwick hadn't been able to stop staring at Kirsty during her evening at Glyndebourne. 'You'd better watch out, Kirsty.'

'Why?'

'He's just at the right age to be having a mid-life crisis. Probably on the hunt for some firm young flesh.'

Kirsty laughed. 'You've got to be kidding. His daughter's nearly as old as I am.'

'You've met his daughter?'

'And his son. Sarah and George—nice kids. I took them skating in the park on Saturday afternoon when James got caught up taking Jade Reynolds off to theatre.'

'James?' Ian echoed again incredulously. He would never in his wildest dreams have been brash enough to call the top consultant for cardiac surgery by his given name.

'He *asked* me to call him James,' Kirsty said defensively. 'I must say I was a bit surprised, myself. And then this was sitting here in the office when I arrived this morning.' Kirsty waved a hand at the large box. 'There was a note saying that the children had enjoyed themselves more than they had in a very long time and were keen to repeat the outing. He said he hopes this gift will encourage me to consider it.'

'Forget the mid-life crisis,' Ian responded acerbically. 'He's after a nanny. What does Mrs Fenwick do?'

'Not much. She died three years ago.' Kirsty had lifted one of the shiny black boots from the box. 'These are amazing. I'm not sure I should accept them.'

'I'm not sure you should, either.' Ian found the sight of the expensive-looking sports gear rather disturbing. He wanted to change the subject. 'You must be glad to be back on early shift.'

'Absolutely!' Kirsty's eyes demonstrated a customary level of sparkle. 'It's a new start. I'm going to pretend that little episode with Signor Tonolo never happened. In fact, I'm planning to celebrate. Are you on tonight?'

'After a whole weekend? Give me a break.'

'How 'bout we get a bottle of wine and listen to some music tonight?'

'Sounds great,' Ian said warmly. 'Your room or mine?'

'Yours,' Kirsty said firmly. 'It's always much tidier.'

Ian's pager sounded and he moved to the phone. His conversation was brief. 'See you later, Kirsty. That was the A and E sister, Maddie Brooks. She's got a sick baby for me to check on.'

Kirsty packed the roller blades away and shifted the

box off Jane's desk. She was a little awed at receiving such attention from James Fenwick. The flowers had been more than enough of an appreciative gesture. Maybe the surgeon cared a great deal for his children and no doubt they had been through a rough time since the death of their mother. Kirsty liked the idea that James would want to provide them with a repeat of an experience they had enjoyed. She was also quite gratified that the children had so obviously liked her. Maybe she would take the roller blades over to the park in the evening and just see whether she might be able to achieve some degree of proficiency.

The in-patient population of the cardiology ward had changed considerably over the week Kirsty had been on night duty. Jamie Bell had been discharged and seemed likely to escape any nasty repercussions from his dose of Kawasaki disease. Harry Wilton was also long gone, having made a brilliant recovery from his bypass surgery. His future also looked brighter—at least in the short term. Jade Reynolds was still in Intensive Care but was showing a slow improvement following the weekend's surgery. The most recent blood culture had been negative and the pericardial drain could possibly be removed tomorrow.

Ian requested Kirsty's assistance when he arrived back in the ward some time later with the six-month-old baby boy he had been to see in A and E.

'This is Oliver Reeves,' he told Kirsty. 'Could you take him into the treatment room, please? I'm just going to find someone to stay with Oliver's parents while we examine him.'

Kirsty took charge of the baby. His mother was clearly distraught and her husband was doing his best to comfort her. It was probably better that they had a short break from any medical intervention their son needed.

Charles Bruce was with Ian when he appeared in the treatment room. Kirsty was still holding the fretting baby.

'He should really be going to ICU,' Ian was saying, 'but they don't have any beds.'

Charles peered at the baby in Kirsty's arms. 'Hello, young man. You're not too happy, are you?' The consultant's kindly face was creased with concern. He looked away to his registrar. 'What's the history?'

'Normal, full-term baby, first child. Birth weight six pounds ten ounces. He was seen at six weeks and the GP noted a slight heart murmur but told the mother not to worry—it was quite common. She missed the next appointment. Oliver's been feeding poorly for the last month since she switched from breast-feeding to a bottle. He hasn't been interested in any solids. In the last week she'd found him soaked with sweat on several occasions. This morning she found him running a fever and breathing so fast she was terrified. They brought him straight in to A and E.'

Charles was watching the baby carefully as Ian spoke. 'He's got intercostal and subcostal retractions with respiration. Has he had a chest X-ray?'

Ian nodded. 'He's got increased pulmonary vascularity with effusion. Possible left lower lobe pneumonia.'

'Has he been seen by Respiratory?'

'Yes. They called us in having found an abnormal cardiothoracic ratio with generalised cardiac enlargement, abnormal second heart sound, a diastolic gallop and a systolic murmur.'

Charles was holding one of Oliver's hands. The baby

protested vigorously. 'No clubbing or oedema,' the consultant noted, 'but there's marked vasoconstriction. His hand's a little block of ice.' He unhooked his stethoscope but looked thoughtful. 'Let's see if we can quieten him down a bit. Try singing to him, Kirsty.'

Kirsty caught Ian's eye. 'I'll just hum,' she decided. She held Oliver close to her body and walked, humming quietly into the baby's ear.

Charles and Ian were looking over the chart that had come up from A and E.

'Heart-rate one eighty, respiration rate seventy-two, BP eighty systolic, unobtainable diastolic. Any bloods been done?'

Ian flipped over the top page of the chart. Biochemistry result forms were clipped underneath. 'White blood count is well up at sixteen thousand. Haemoglobin is well down—he's very anaemic.'

'ECG?'

Kirsty listened as Ian produced the heart trace and the doctors discussed the abnormal findings. Oliver was finally beginning to settle.

'We'll need an echo.' Charles nodded. 'I'd say we're probably looking at a ventricular septal defect.' He smiled at Kirsty. 'Keep holding him, Kirsty, but see if you can turn him sideways a bit without upsetting him. That way I can have a listen to his chest.'

'What about an arterial blood gas sample?' Ian queried when Charles had finished.

'Good idea,' the consultant responded. 'I'll leave that to you and Kirsty. Has blood gone for cultures?'

'Yes. Nothing back yet, of course.'

'We'll start antibiotics, IV and maintenance fluids. Lasix and digoxin. Give half the digoxin IV as a loading dose, the other two quarters at six-hourly intervals—the usual protocol with a rhythm strip before each dose to check for toxicity. Let's get his oxygen saturation up. I don't like this dusky colour. We'd better consider a packed cell transfusion as well, to deal with the anaemia.' Charles moved towards the door. 'Call me as soon as you get the echo results. I'll go and talk to his parents.'

Ian smiled at Oliver as Dr Bruce left. 'Sorry about this, wee man. I'm going to have to upset you just when you've decided you like Nurse Kirsty.'

'Where are you going to take the sample?' Kirsty asked. 'He's pretty shut down peripherally.'

'I guess we'll go for a femoral stab.' Ian sighed. 'I hate doing this.'

Kirsty cuddled the baby. 'So do I.'

'I'll get Jane to come in and help restrain him. Can you get the trolley set up?'

Kirsty nodded. 'You'll want an IV tray as well, won't you?'

'Yes, thanks. We'll get started on the medications immediately. We'll need to set up an oxygen tent too. Should keep us out of mischief for a while.'

In fact, young Oliver Reeves kept Kirsty and Ian out of mischief for most of the day. The echo confirmed the cardiac abnormality but the hole in his heart was not large. The heart failure had probably been precipitated by the pneumonia and made worse by the anaemia. Oliver needed constant monitoring throughout Kirsty's shift and she stayed later to make sure the nurse taking over from her was completely confident of continuing the same level of observation and care.

Kirsty was limping slightly when she entered Ian's room that evening.

'I fell over,' she explained, prompted by Ian's concerned query. 'Skating.'

'Oh. So you decided to keep them, then.'

Kirsty ignored the overtone of disapproval. She produced a bottle from behind her back. 'Look at this, Jimmy!'

'Champagne—wow!'

'I told you I was celebrating.'

'You didn't tell me you were buying.' Ian shook his head. 'I guess we don't have to drink the stuff I got.'

'What did *you* get?'

'A nice white and some red. I wasn't sure what you'd prefer.'

'Have you got any food?'

'Peanuts and crisps,' Ian confirmed. 'And I've got some glasses from the kitchen.'

Kirsty was struggling with the wire holding the champagne cork in place.

'I'll do that,' Ian offered. 'You choose some music.' He offered Kirsty a large tumbler full of sparkling golden liquid. 'What shall we drink to?'

'Life,' Kirsty said with determination.

'Here's to it,' Ian agreed. 'It sure beats the hell out of the alternative.'

Kirsty had finished her glass of champagne by the time Ian was halfway through his. She finished her second glass as Ian opened the last bag of crisps.

'My mother was right. Scottish blood is ninety per cent proof most of the time.'

'Aye, well, we need the alcohol to keep the damp from creeping up our kilts.' Kirsty was sprawled on Ian's bed, propped up on one elbow.

'I thought it was only the men who wore the kilts.'

'Och, aye.' Kirsty giggled. 'And do you know what they wear underneath them?'

'No. Do you?'

'No.' Kirsty sighed wistfully. 'I think I'll try and find out.' She held up her glass. 'Fill it up, Jimmy!'

'Are you sure you want to? Why don't you have something to eat?'

Kirsty gave Ian a stern look. 'Of course I'm sure. I'm all grown up, Ian. I've even got a failed romance under my belt.' She was silent for a moment and then her face brightened. 'Can I see your bagpipes?'

'Sure.' Ian pulled a rectangular wooden box out from under his bed and opened the lid carefully. 'These belonged to my great-grandfather,' he told Kirsty proudly. She peered at the contents of the box. The bag was made of a tartan material; the pipes were lying at odd angles on top of it. She giggled again.

'Looks like an octopus with rigor mortis. Play something, Ian.'

'No way. It's far too loud. Anyway, I've got to redo all the hemp some time. I'd never be able to tune it at the moment. The reed on the chanter needs changing, too.' Ian was touching the wooden pipes reverently. 'These are made of ebony, you know, and that's real sterling silver. My great-grandfather brought them out from Scotland when he emigrated to New Zealand. I only met him once. All I can remember are these amazingly knobbly knees under his kilt. He never wore anything else. I was quite convinced he slept in it.'

Kirsty appeared to be fascinated and Ian felt encouraged. 'This is the practice chanter.' He held up the slim pipe for her inspection. 'It's a lot quieter than the real thing. The reed's a bit stuffed on this one as well but I could play you something, if you like.'

'OK. I'll get myself another glass of champagne.' Kirsty leaned over the side of the bed. 'Ian!' she said accusingly. 'You've drunk it all!' Kirsty sighed dramatically. 'And they say Scots drink like fish. They don't know about you Kiwis. Let's try the white.'

'Not a good idea.' Ian was already feeling the effects from half the amount of champagne that Kirsty had put away. She had to be flying quite high enough.

'The red, then.'

'Even worse.'

'I know!' Kirsty's eyes were shining. 'Let's mix them together and have some *pink* wine.'

Ian had to laugh. She was quite irresistible. 'I guess one glass of white wouldn't hurt.'

'You're an angel, Ian. I love you.'

'I love you, too. Try and drink this one a bit more slowly, OK?'

'OK.' Kirsty took a large gulp of the white wine.

Ian knew it had been a mistake to open the bottle. He abandoned his glass in favour of demonstrating his chanter to Kirsty.

'This tune is called "Chasing Shadows". It's a nice fast hornpipe. I used to be able to play it quite well but I'm out of practice now.' Ian blew enthusiastically, his fingers moving over the holes with a graceful skill. The quality of sound was well removed from the level of dexterity Ian displayed, however.

'It's awful!' Kirsty cried happily. 'Can I have a go?'

Kirsty got to her feet somewhat unsteadily. She blew eagerly on the chanter but couldn't make a single sound. Her face became alarmingly red.

'It takes a bit of practice.' Ian reached out to take the chanter back and rescue Kirsty's blood pressure.

Somehow, he found himself holding Kirsty as well as the chanter.

'I love you, Ian,' Kirsty stated fondly. Her words were distinctly blurred. 'You're the besht friend I've ever had.'

Ian just smiled. He held Kirsty a little tighter as he felt her body slump against his.

'Make love to me, Ian.'

'Not right now.' Ian took a deep breath. His body was doing its best to let him know that the idea had certain merits.

'Nobody lovsh me.' Kirsty's blue eyes filled with sudden tears. 'I'm shtill going to be a virgin when I'm shixty.' She tried to look up at Ian's face but her neck was having difficulty supporting her head. 'Itsh becaush I've got red hair, ishn't it?'

'No. It's because you're as drunk as a lord,' Ian told her. 'I'm not going to take advantage of you.' Much as I'd like to, he added silently.

Kirsty didn't appear to have heard him. She had subsided into an uneasy silence.

'Ian?'

'Yes, Kirsty.'

'I feel shick.'

'I'm not surprised.'

There was another short silence.

'Ian?'

'Yes, Kirsty.'

'I feel *very* shick.'

Kirsty's proof of the way she was feeling was dramatically rapid. Ian sighed. So much for the new level of maturity. He took Kirsty into his bathroom and washed her face. Then he undressed her and put her into one of his clean T-shirts.

'Come and get into bed, Kirsty.'

'Oh, no.' Kirsty wagged her head dubiously. 'I don't feel well enough for that any more, Ian.' She hiccuped and turned even paler. 'I'm dying.'

'No. You only wish you were.' Ian put his arm around Kirsty and lifted her easily. He put her into his bed and pulled the covers up. She was snoring loudly by the time he had tucked her in.

Ian cleaned up his room and drank several large glasses of water in an attempt to ward off a possible hangover. Then he settled himself into the single arm-chair his room provided and gazed at the bundle of red curls occupying his pillow. Thank goodness he had controlled his own alcoholic intake. Any more and he would probably have been unable to refuse her invitation. They would have both regretted the hasty change in their relationship and that would have been that.

Kirsty would have confirmed her belief that romance and friendship couldn't co-exist and Ian would have lost both her trust and the tenuous hope he still had of a future together. Ian was patient. He could wait until the timing was perfect.

Kirsty McTavish was a sorry sight. Ian silently handed her a couple of aspirin and a large glass of water when he found her in the kitchen while he was on his coffee break.

'Drink it all,' he advised. 'You're dehydrated. It makes the headache worse.'

'I'll never drink again,' Kirsty told him in a hollow voice. 'I've taken the pledge.' She shut her eyes as she swallowed the tablets, then she peered at Ian. 'Where were you this morning?'

'I went for a run. I thought you might want a shower in peace.'

'Oh...thanks.' Kirsty looked away. 'I don't remember getting into bed last night.'

'You needed a wee bit of help,' Ian said kindly.

'Oh.' Kirsty's cheeks gained a little colour which did wonders for her general appearance. 'Um...thanks, Ian.'

'Don't mention it. What are friends for?'

Jane Armstrong entered the kitchen. She clicked her tongue. 'You look dreadful, Kirsty. I hope you're not coming down with something.' Jane turned her attention to Ian before Kirsty needed to reply. 'Have you seen Oliver Reeves this morning?'

Ian nodded. 'Blood cultures are negative. Arterial blood gas normal on room air. Weight's dropped ten ounces. Heart-rate, temperature and respiration rate are all down a bit. Blood pressure up. He's still pale but not dusky and his pulses are good. Haemoglobin's still too low.'

'Digoxin levels?'

'Good. I'm just going to chart a maintenance dose at thirty per cent of his loading dose. It'll need to be intra-muscular when we discontinue his IV line. So will the antibiotics, I'm afraid. I want to get a packed cell transfusion in first, though.'

'Can you look after that, Kirsty?' Jane gave her junior nurse a sharp glance.

'Of course.' Kirsty tipped the rest of her glass of water into the sink.

'It needs to be slow,' Ian advised. 'Five ml per kilogram. I'll help you set up the pump. He can be started on clear fluids now, too. If he tolerates that we'll start a formula with added iron.'

Kirsty was feeling quite a lot better by lunch-time.

She still eyed the paper bag Ian was offering her with some suspicion.

'If it's food, forget it.'

'It's only a sandwich from the cafeteria. You're on your lunch break, aren't you?'

Kirsty wasn't looking at the bag any more. She was staring past Ian's shoulder. The change in her expression prompted Ian to turn his head.

'Mr Fenwick! Is there something I can help you with?'

James Fenwick gave Ian a perfunctory nod but his eyes were on Kirsty. 'It's Nurse McTavish I came to see. Are you busy at the moment, Kirsty?'

'No, I'm on my lunch break. I've got half an hour.'

'Good.' James Fenwick gave another brief nod. 'So am I. If you'll allow me to accompany you, perhaps we could come to some arrangement that might stop my children nagging me so much at breakfast.' The consultant gazed down the corridor towards the ward office. 'I'll have a word with your charge nurse and see if we can extend your lunch break enough to visit a little outdoor bistro nearby. The food in the cafeteria is appalling, don't you think?'

'Mmm.' Kirsty's response sounded a little strangled. She didn't appear to notice Ian squashing the paper bag he held into a soggy wad.

Chapter Six

THE outing with the Fenwick family was something of a revelation.

Kirsty had escaped as her shift had ended on Saturday afternoon, changed and tidied herself with determined swiftness and was waiting, as arranged, outside Lizzie's staff quarters building at four p.m. The laces of her roller blades were knotted and looped over her shoulder. The unseasonable warmth of the October afternoon promised a couple more hours of enjoyable time to spend outdoors. Kirsty craned her neck a little, her eyes scanning the windows of the third floor. She smiled happily and waved when she saw Ian Fraser standing at his window, but the wave was not returned.

Had he not seen her or was he miffed that she hadn't told him about her excursion? The noises coming from his room had indicated a resolved attempt to master 'Changing Shadows' and Kirsty hadn't wanted to interrupt. The disappointment at not being acknowledged was short-lived. It vanished as the silver Daimler cruised to a halt beside her and the driver stepped out. Kirsty reached for the passenger door handle but James Fenwick's hand reached it first.

'Allow me,' he murmured, smiling courteously.

'Thanks.' Kirsty sank into the luxurious leather upholstery. 'Ooch!' she exclaimed loudly. She fished the roller blade out from behind her back as George giggled in the back seat. James Fenwick's hand was again outstretched, this time to remove her awkward burden, and Kirsty obediently handed the boots over. She hoped she hadn't damaged the upholstery. As James put the roller blades into the boot of the car, Kirsty twisted around to smile at the children. Her mouth dropped open.

'Sarah! What *have* you done to your hair?'

The teenager had been a brunette the last time she'd seen her. Now her short, spiky hair was a startlingly vivid shade of red.

James Fenwick slid behind the wheel of the car. 'I told you you'd made an impression, Kirsty.' He glanced in the rear-view mirror at his daughter as he eased the large vehicle into the flow of traffic, and he shook his head in bewildered resignation. 'What can one do?'

'I like it,' Kirsty stated, earning a smile from Sarah and a surprised glance from James. 'The best thing about hair is that it keeps growing. You get any number of opportunities to try something new.' She glanced at James Fenwick's full head of dark hair. The grey was only obvious when you looked closely and it went with the dignified image the surgeon projected so effortlessly. Kirsty looked into the back seat again. 'What's it going to be next time, Sarah?'

'Hmm. Green, I think.'

James Fenwick's laugh was not particularly amused. 'Perhaps red isn't so bad, after all.'

Hyde Park was an interesting change for Kirsty. With Regent's Park being so close to Lizzie's, she and Ian now knew it extremely well. The times they had ventured further afield, they had always picked destinations of the more popular tourist attractions like Westminster Cathedral, the Tower of London, Madame Tussaud's and the British Museum. Hyde Park was new territory for Kirsty and on an early Saturday evening it was a vibrant place to be.

Speakers' Corner was packed. An elderly man with a long, unkempt white beard was proclaiming, amongst much good-natured heckling, that the end of the world was due on October thirty-first.

'So much for the staff association's Halloween Ball.' Kirsty grinned. 'Perhaps I'd better not bother hiring a costume.'

'What are you going as?' George asked with interest.

'I'm not sure yet. A witch, I guess.' Kirsty winked at Sarah. 'It would give me a good excuse to dye my hair black.'

Sarah fingered her own spiky hair thoughtfully. She turned to her father. 'What are you going as, Dad?'

'I doubt very much that I'll attend.' James Fenwick was offhand. 'Dressing up's not really my scene. I'll wait till the formal Christmas Ball in December. That should be somewhat more civilised.'

Kirsty glanced at the consultant. He appeared to have made an effort to dress casually but the pale linen trousers and navy-blue blazer still came across as rather formal. Kirsty was glad she had worn her own smartly tailored brown jacket over her jeans and silk shirt. The children were both dressed in baggy cargo pants and oversized T-shirts. James was the only one not wearing well-scuffed trainers. No, she couldn't really see him in fancy dress at a riotous hospital function.

Sarah had looked disappointed but then nodded as though the response from her father had been what she had expected. George had started using his skateboard but now jumped off it and tucked it under his arm.

'Can I have a go on your roller blades, Sarah?'

'Roller balls,' Sarah corrected. 'And, no, you can't.

They'd be miles too big for you and I don't want them wrecked.'

Kirsty ignored the brief squabble that ensued between the siblings. There were any number of distractions. The park was crowded. People walked their dogs, jogged and power-walked and roller-blading was popular. The lake had attracted a model boat club that was holding some sort of regatta and they were competing for space with swimmers and larger boats with real people inside. Family groups were everywhere. Picnicking, playing cricket and soccer, throwing Frisbees and riding bicycles. Kirsty found the atmosphere something quite new.

It was the first time Kirsty had ever been out with a real family group. She had never known her own father and she had been an only child. Now she was included in a group that was typical of the divisions amongst the crowd in Hyde Park that evening, even down to a pair of argumentative children. All they needed was a dog to complete the portrait. Kirsty was enjoying the new experience although it evoked a certain wistfulness as it emphasised what her own childhood had lacked.

George was sulking. Sarah was looking smug. 'This looks like a great place to skate, Kirsty. Let's put our roller blades on.'

'Balls,' muttered George. He looked ready to burst into tears. Kirsty was about to offer to roll up her socks and stuff them into the toes of her boots so he could try them when George himself provided the solution.

'Look at that kiosk! They're hiring roller blades. Can I get some, Dad? Can I? *Please*?'

'Why not?' James agreed tolerantly. 'Anything for a peaceful life.'

'You could hire some too, James.' Kirsty bit her lip

as the impulsive words left her mouth. The momentary stunned silence that greeted the suggestion made her quite aware that a soon-to-be-knighted consultant cardiac surgeon was highly unlikely to contemplate gliding around Hyde Park on a pair of roller blades.

'Why not?' James Fenwick's relaxed response caused the children to gape at their father. Then they turned astonished gazes towards Kirsty. 'Just don't let me break any limbs,' James added thoughtfully.

The owner of Cheapskates Skate Hire was quite happy to look after George's skateboard and the jackets of both James and Kirsty. Within minutes the small group was cautiously advancing along a fortunately unpopular pathway. Sarah was way out in front but George fearlessly increased his speed. Kirsty felt a lot more confident now but she matched her initial pace to James Fenwick's tentative speed. She was delighted to see that the surgeon at least had a good sense of balance. She would have been mortified if her suggestion had led to an undignified fall.

'It's not so different to ice-skating,' he commented after concentrating silently for several minutes. 'I used to do quite a lot of that during holidays in Switzerland. A long time ago,' he added dryly. 'Part of my uninhibited youth.'

The skills seemed to return quickly. Even when they began to negotiate a more heavily populated pathway they met with no disasters. The children were shouting gleefully as they repeatedly passed each other and Kirsty had to put on a burst of speed to even catch up with James. He glanced back at her, slowed and then stopped, tipping alarmingly to regain his balance once stationary.

'James!'

Kirsty was still several yards away. She saw the middle-aged couple stop beside James, their immaculately clipped standard poodle dropping instantly to a sitting position beside them.

'Sir Brian.' James Fenwick nodded at the older man, whose double-breasted pinstriped suit jacket sported a white carnation in its buttonhole. 'And Lady Dunlop.' The woman's hair had a mauve tinge and it was trimmed as perfectly as their poodle's traditional lion cut. 'A pleasure,' James Fenwick finished blandly. 'Such a nice day, isn't it?'

Kirsty caught up with James, having been apparently invisible to the Dunlops.

'I'll be the talk of the Club next week,' James told her wryly. He looked down at his feet. His linen trousers had been stuffed into the top of the roller-blade boots.

'I'm sorry,' Kirsty apologised. 'Maybe it wasn't such a good idea.'

'It was a great idea,' James said firmly. 'I've enjoyed myself immensely and I'm not at all sorry.' He leaned a little closer to Kirsty. 'Confidentially, I've always found Sir Brian something of a stuffed shirt!'

'Oh!' Kirsty didn't know how to respond. She caught her companion's eye a little tentatively.

'Do you think,' James continued seriously, 'that Lady Dunlop takes her dog to her hairdresser? Or does she, in fact, attend the poodle parlour?'

Kirsty burst into laughter. James Fenwick was actually a very nice man, she decided. Very nice indeed.

'He's very nice, Ian. Not a bit stuffy. And he's very good at roller-blading.'

Ian's expression was supremely unimpressed. 'All I

meant was that I'm sure the future Lady Fenwick wouldn't recognise a pair of roller blades if they landed in her platter of smoked salmon!'

'Well, I'm not remotely interested in becoming *Lady* Fenwick,' Kirsty retorted. She paused. 'It does have kind of a romantic ring to it, though, doesn't it?'

'Oh, God,' Ian groaned. 'Pass me that urine analysis form, will you?' He ticked several boxes and then scrawled his signature at the bottom. 'Are you sure you're confident of getting a clean urine sample from a ten-month-old girl, Kirsty?'

'Of course. I'll even deliver it to the lab for you within the hour.'

'Good. Hey, have you hired your costume for the Halloween Ball yet?'

'No. Have you?'

'I'm going this afternoon. What do you think I should go as?'

'Save yourself some money and go as Frankenstein,' Kirsty suggested. 'All you need are a couple of plastic bolts to stick on your neck.'

'Thanks, Kirsty.' Ian walked off, shaking his head. 'I think you should go as a goblin.'

The time limit for the urine sample had been a challenge. Kirsty washed the baby and thought she had dried the skin thoroughly but the sticky material around the top of the specially designed plastic collection bag adhered only long enough for Kirsty to pick up the clean nappy. The second one adhered quite well but the baby managed to grab hold of it as Kirsty lifted her legs to slide the nappy underneath. She waved it triumphantly in a fat little fist.

Kirsty had to rush back to the supply room to obtain another collection bag. She hoped, desperately, that the baby wouldn't choose her absence to relieve her bladder. The fluid loading Kirsty had persuaded her to drink thirty minutes ago had been quite an effort. She was very keen to complete this task successfully and save the baby the trauma of a suprapubic stab to obtain the sample urgently needed to test her renal function.

Kirsty's third attempt was successful, having gained the mother's assistance in keeping young Emma's hands out of the way. Kirsty carefully put a disposable nappy on her and cut a slit in the front to ease the bag through. This allowed room for the urine to collect and enabled the rapid removal of the bag as soon as the specimen was available. The moisture could easily loosen the adhesive and the sample would be lost if not removed immediately.

Kirsty held the baby, walking her around the room and jiggling her up and down in the hope of applying some gentle pressure over her bladder. After ten minutes she wished she hadn't been so hasty in promising Ian a time of arrival. She turned the tap on over the sink.

'Works for me, Emma.' Kirsty grinned at Emma's mother. 'In fact, it's working for me right now. What is it about the sound of running water, do you think?'

Whatever it was, it seemed to do the trick for Emma as well. Kirsty raced off to the lab with the sample and then visited a nearby staff toilet before retracing her path through the hospital. The sight of Paolo Tonolo standing in front of a lift gave Kirsty an unpleasant surprise. She had forgotten that the surgical registrar was due back at work this week. He was not alone. Kirsty smiled warmly at James Fenwick.

'Thanks so much for last night, James. I haven't enjoyed myself so much for a long time.' Kirsty was gratified at the stunned expression on Paolo's face that she caught out of the corner of her eye.

'Neither had we.' James was smiling. A group of senior staff members passed by and all nodded towards the surgeon. Kirsty could feel their respect. It enclosed James Fenwick like a bubble. A bubble she was also standing inside. The feeling was quite alien but not at all unpleasant. Kirsty straightened her spine a little.

'I'm sorry we made such a mess in your kitchen cooking the pancakes. I hope your housekeeper wasn't too upset.'

'She coped. And even if she hadn't the experience would have been well worth while.'

'And I'm sorry I embarrassed you in the park.' Kirsty lowered her voice, shooting a quick glance at Paolo who appeared riveted by their conversation. 'I know some people consider me a little immature at times.'

'Not at all.' James Fenwick was still smiling. 'It's time I was reminded that I'm not old enough to have forgotten what it's like to have fun. You achieved something my children have been attempting for years. We're all grateful.'

Kirsty tilted her head in pleased acknowledgement. The lift doors finally opened for the surgeons and they took their leave. Paolo had said nothing but he was gazing at Kirsty with a new respect.

Kirsty gazed at her reflection in her bathroom mirror with a new respect herself later that afternoon. The flattened hairstyle she had perfected on her week of night duty made her look older and much more dignified. The transformation the suit gave her image was nothing short of dramatic. She had purchased the suit, in a shade of rich chestnut brown, for her mother's funeral and had only worn the tailored jacket since, to dress up her jeans. Teamed with the equally well-tailored skirt and the cream silk blouse, it was elegantly sophisticated, Kirsty knew. The single string of pearls that she had inherited from her mother was a fitting final touch.

The only knock to the confidence the mirror had engendered came from meeting Ian Fraser as she left her room.

'Lady Fenwick!' Ian tugged on the curls above his forehead.

'Don't be nasty, Ian. We're just going out to tea, that's all. I wanted to see if I could look a little less scruffy than usual.'

'High tea, is it? Cucumber sandwiches and crumpets. You'll be the crumpet if you're not careful, Kirsty McTavish.'

'Don't be ridiculous.' Kirsty was beginning to get irritated by Ian's attitude. 'It's Sarah's birthday and it's only afternoon tea.'

'You'll be an evil stepmother before you know it.'

'I have no intention of becoming a stepmother. I intend to have my *own* babies, thank you!'

Kirsty stalked off, annoyed that she had allowed Ian to draw her into an argument yet again. Why did she feel the need to defend herself so often lately? Just because he had taken care of her when she'd thrown up all over his room didn't give him the right to be quite so possessive. Something had changed subtly in their relationship that night and Kirsty didn't feel happy about it. She could remember that evening quite clearly up until the time she had suddenly become so unwell. She remembered the surge of desire she had felt in Ian's arms. And she remembered, only too well, his total lack of interest. It was embarrassing. Thank goodness he hadn't taken pity on her and accepted her offer.

Kirsty needed a boost to her self-image. Even being in the courteous and charming company that James Fenwick provided did wonders for her. The new respect with which some members of Lizzie's staff regarded her, having seen her in the consultant's company, was another, even more noticeable boost. And as for the glances Paolo Tonolo bestowed upon her! The Italian registrar clearly hankered over what he had missed out on but even he wouldn't try to step in front of James Fenwick. They all had the wrong impression, of course. James wasn't interested in her in any romantic sense. But it was rather nice that people made the assumption that he could be.

Jade Reynolds wasn't coming back to the ward. The signs of improvement after her surgery had not lasted more than a day or two. Her heart failure had become progressively more difficult to manage and the ability of her liver and kidneys to function was deteriorating rapidly. Ian Fraser broke the news to Kirsty the day after her outing for Sarah Fenwick's birthday. Jane Armstrong was also present. They both looked at Kirsty's pale, still face with concern.

'I'm sorry, Kirsty,' Ian said gently. 'I know how fond of Jade you are.'

'I thought...I hoped...'

'I know.' Ian put his arm around Kirsty's shoulders. 'Her heart was already badly damaged. The infection on top of that has just been too much.'

'How's Barbara?' Kirsty's face was twisted in an effort to control incipient tears.

'Remarkably calm,' Ian told her. 'They've taken all Jade's lines out. The boys have all been in to say goodbye. She has both her parents with her now.'

Kirsty's lip trembled.

'Would you like to go and see them?' Jane asked quietly. 'You don't need to come back today. I'll find someone to cover the rest of your shift.'

Kirsty nodded. She didn't trust herself to speak. Ian took her hand and held it all the way to the intensive care unit. Jade had been transferred into a private, single room. The curtains had been half closed.

'The light was hurting her eyes,' Barbara explained. 'She can't see terribly well any more. Come up close, Kirsty. She may still be able to hear you.'

Kirsty moved slowly nearer the bed. Ian had gone. Barbara lay beside her daughter, holding the frail child in her arms. Her husband sat beside them, one arm around his wife, the other holding Jade's hand.

'I don't want to intrude,' Kirsty whispered. 'I just wanted...' Her voice caught and she rubbed at the sudden tears that escaped with her fist. Nobody else was crying. There was a curiously peaceful atmosphere in the room. Jade was enclosed in the comfort of her parents' love and Kirsty felt she had no real business to be here at all. But Barbara Reynolds smiled.

'It's lovely that you care so much, Kirsty. Jade was very fond of you, too. The more love there is in this room at the moment, the better. Don't go just yet.'

Kirsty took another tentative step forward. The ICU nurse who was unobtrusively providing care for Jade stepped back having smoothed some salve onto the child's cracked lips. Kirsty reached out and traced a finger gently over Jade's forehead, straightening the wisps of blonde hair. Then she leaned forward and kissed her softly. She doubted that Jade was even aware of her presence. A Cheyne-Stokes respiratory pattern was evident, the depth of her breathing showing marked variation with regular periods of the efforts ceasing completely. Kirsty stood for a minute and became aware of the rattle starting in Jade's breath sounds.

The death rattle. Kirsty recognised it immediately. For an instant she was back beside her mother's bed, being swept inevitably towards their final parting. That death had been expected—a release, although that hadn't made it seem any easier at the time. Jade was only a child. It was infinitely harder.

Kirsty could see the nurse drawing up a syringe of atropine which would lessen the rattle. While the build-up of secretions would not bother Jade, it would be very distressing for her parents. Kirsty's vision blurred and somehow she excused herself. Blindly stumbling from the room, she walked straight into the person standing outside. As she drew ragged breaths and tried to block her tears with her hands Kirsty felt strong masculine arms enfold her. It should be Ian, Kirsty thought wildly. He would understand. She *needed* Ian.

But James Fenwick seemed just as capable of administering comfort. Kirsty found herself in his office within minutes, encouraged to express her grief and offered numerous tissues. It was a new side to the consultant surgeon and Kirsty felt enormously grateful.

'I'm sorry,' she said eventually. 'I should be able to cope better than this. It's part of my job.'

'Part of what makes you so good at your job is the fact that you care so much,' James responded. 'Unfortunately, you'll learn to protect yourself by becoming less involved, as we all learn to do.' He was watching

Kirsty with gentle concern. 'It's good to be reminded sometimes of what we're really here for.'

'I'd better go,' Kirsty told him.

'Not back on duty, I hope?'

'No. Jane said I didn't need to. I'd like to get away from Lizzie's for a bit, I think.'

'Pack some clothes,' James suggested. 'Come back to my house for a few days.'

The invitation was astounding. Kirsty's startled gaze flew to meet James Fenwick's eyes.

'The staff quarters are not going to be much of a change in atmosphere for you, Kirsty. Being in the company of a couple of lively and argumentative children probably would. I won't be there. I'm flying out this afternoon for a conference in Beijing.'

Kirsty blinked. 'It's very kind of you, James, but I'm not sure—'

James cut off her protest. 'That's settled, then. You go and get organised and I'll collect you outside the door in—' he glanced at his watch '—forty five minutes.'

The change was exactly what Kirsty needed. Her gratitude for the surgeon's sensitivity increased as she recognised just how beneficial the family environment was. Mrs Benny was not the ogre the children had implied. She welcomed Kirsty and fussed over her as though she were Sarah's age. The house and lifestyle were just as luxurious as Paolo's but the presence of the children ensured that Kirsty didn't feel intimidated.

Kirsty used the underground to get from Knightsbridge to Lizzie's, getting off at Baker Street and walking the rest of the way. She helped George with his homework after school, spent time analysing fashion, hairstyles and colouring techniques to Sarah's satisfaction, took the children skating and spent the evenings watching television with them, having initi-ated them into the secrets of making good popcorn. Kirsty found she was looking forward to finishing each shift at Lizzie's—a fact that had not gone unnoticed by Ian Fraser.

Ian had received the information of Kirsty's visit to the Fenwick house quietly. Too quietly. Kirsty found that his unspoken disapproval made her feel guilty and for the first time she actually began to subtly avoid his company on the ward, timing her breaks for when he was absent or caught up with a patient. He helped her by requesting assistance from other staff members when needed and perversely this made Kirsty cross. *She* was the one avoiding *him*—not the reverse.

Kirsty planned to go back to the staff quarters on the afternoon of James' return from China, having stayed at the Fenwick house for almost a week. It wouldn't be acceptable to sleep under the same roof, no matter how platonic their relationship. The call from James at lunch-time was a surprise. He was back in London and had gone straight to Lizzie's. His invita-tion to dinner was even more of a surprise.

'Mrs Benny tells me you're heading back to the staff quarters this afternoon. I'll pick you up at seven-thirty after I've seen the children.'

Kirsty's response was a confused stammer. James laughed.

'Wear that lovely black dress you wore to Glyndebourne,' he instructed. 'We'll go somewhere nice.'

Fortunately, Ian didn't witness Kirsty's exit after her efforts to achieve 'especially elegant' for the second time. The Daimler was just as appropriate as the chauffeured limousine for her successful result and Kirsty thought it was quite possible that she could become used to the routine. While nervous of this unexpected development in her relationship with James Fenwick, Kirsty was glad of the opportunity to thank him.

'It was exactly what I needed,' she confided, taking a very cautious sip from her glass of champagne. Their table at the Savoy was in a discreet corner of the dining room and the setting was as glamorous as James Fenwick in evening attire. 'I've never felt like part of a family before. It was very special. I'd like to thank you for your kindness.'

'My pleasure.' James Fenwick's smile was warm.

Surprisingly, conversation was easy even without the children present. The food was wonderful and, although Kirsty made sure she drank a lot of water, the level in her wine glass still seemed to need frequent replenishment. Kirsty was eager to hear about the conference in China and the other exotic locations James had travelled to recently.

'I'd *love* to travel,' she confessed. 'You see some amazing places. China, Russia, Argentina and where was the last one?'

'Barbados.' James shrugged. 'The interest in locations isn't really there when you travel alone.' The long glance he gave Kirsty was meaningful enough to quicken her pulse considerably. She took a larger gulp of wine. James smiled.

'Sarah and George tell me they've enjoyed your company immensely over the last few days.'

'They're wonderful children.'

'They've been happier just recently than they have been since the death of their mother. I think they'd be very keen to make it a permanent arrangement.'

Kirsty was stunned. Was this an offer to *adopt* her? She tried to concentrate on what James Fenwick was saying.

'I find your company enchanting, Kirsty. I'm rather afraid I've fallen in love with you.'

Kirsty watched in disbelief as he reached into the pocket of his dinner jacket and produced a small velvet box. He was still talking as he laid it on the table between them.

'I would like you to think about this carefully, Kirsty. I don't expect an answer yet. I do know the difference in our ages could be important to you.' His gaze was very warm. 'Though when I'm with you I don't feel a day over twenty-five.' He was fiddling with the velvet box. It opened slowly.

The solitaire diamond was square-cut and modern. It was also enormous. The fortune it represented made Kirsty all too aware of the position this man held. Wealth, power, influence…and he wanted *her*! It was unbelievable. But James Fenwick also represented security. Maturity and a base that had given her a taste of what family was really about. Kirsty reached out to touch the ring.

'It's too much,' she breathed. 'Are you sure about this, James? I mean, I'm not very…' Kirsty searched for the most important item on her list of inadequacies.

'You're everything you need to be, Kirsty. And more. With you, I get the chance to rediscover things. To re-experience the best of what I thought I'd left behind.'

'But…you haven't even *kissed* me!' Kirsty blurted.

James rose to his feet smoothly. He pulled Kirsty's chair back and took her hands to ease her to her feet. Then, still holding her hands, he bent and touched her lips with his own. He dropped her hands and took hold of her shoulders. The gentle kiss developed into a firm possession of her mouth. His confidence was overpowering, his willingness to make a public scene daring, the touch of his lips and hands wildly exciting. The words leapt from Kirsty's lips as soon as they were released.

'Yes. I'd love to accept your ring, James. I'd love to marry you.'

His eyes were hooded with satisfaction. 'You don't have to wear it just yet,' he advised. 'I won't say anything to the children. I want you to think about it very carefully for at least twenty-four hours.'

Kirsty stood on the front steps of the staff quarters, clutching the little velvet box in her hand, watching the tail-lights of the Daimler disappearing into the traffic. She didn't need twenty-four hours but of course she would think about it carefully.

Kirsty wasn't about to be swept off her feet again, though it felt, right now, as though her feet were having difficulty maintaining contact with the steps. Kirsty was floating. The excitement of a new plot was unfolding. James wasn't just interested in her body. He had proposed to her before he had even *touched* her.

How much more romantic could it get?

Chapter Seven

THE tail-lights of James Fenwick's Daimler had only just become indistinguishable from the surrounding traffic when another vehicle rolled to a halt beside Kirsty McTavish.

A silver Porsche this time. Kirsty cast it an admiring glance before turning towards the door of the staff quarters. Kirsty wondered, briefly, who was being returned from a date with someone wealthy enough to drive such an ostentatious car. The identity hadn't reached the gossip grapevine as yet.

'Kirsty—*cara*! Don't go!' A car door slammed and then Paolo Tonolo was on the steps beside her.

Kirsty's hand fell from the door handle as Paolo grasped both her shoulders and turned her towards him. Before she had any chance to protest her lips were covered. Paolo's mouth was hungry—the onslaught to her senses tinged with desperation. Kirsty didn't try to pull away. She couldn't. Paolo's hands had moved up to cradle her head, holding it firmly as his mouth devoured hers. It made the kiss she had just received from James Fenwick pale to the point of boredom in comparison. *This* was passion!

Finally, Kirsty could breathe again, but Paolo was still holding her head.

'I love you, Kirsty,' Paolo said urgently. 'I don't want to live without you. I *cannot*!' The liquid brown eyes suggested that he would hurl himself off any available cliff as soon as possible if Kirsty turned him down. His lips touched hers again, more gently this time, begging a response. Kirsty closed her eyes. *This* was the stuff of romance. A man ready to die if she refused him. How could she not respond?

'Marry me, Kirsty. I love only you. We will be so happy. We will have *tanti bei bambini.*'

'Bambini?' It sounded like a variety of snack food.

'Babies, my darling. Many beautiful babies. I want to make love to you. I want to make a baby—tonight! Tomorrow! For ever!'

Kirsty's feet began to touch earth. 'You're already getting married,' she pointed out breathlessly. 'To Chantelle.'

'Poof!' Paolo made a wonderfully exotic expression of dismissal. 'Chantelle is history. It's *you* I want, Kirsty. *Only* you.'

'Oh...but...' Kirsty was caught, impaled by the adoration Paolo's gaze bestowed. Her fingers curled more tightly around the small velvet box she was still clutching. 'It's not possible, Paolo. I—'

'Anything is possible with true love. *Everything.*' Paolo was kissing the side of her neck. Kirsty's head tipped back involuntarily.

'True love,' she murmured. 'Oh, yes, Paolo!'

'Yes?' Paolo's head reared back. 'You say yes, *amore mio*? *Dio mio*, I am so happy.' His body twisted elegantly as he slid his hand into the back pocket of a very tight pair of black jeans. He extracted, with some difficulty, a small velvet box. He flicked it open and Kirsty gasped. The enormous round sapphire surrounded by petals of diamonds had to be the largest engagement ring she had ever seen.

Paolo grasped Kirsty's left hand. Fortunately, she was holding the other velvet box in her right hand which she snaked behind her back. Things were way past any control she might have exerted. The ring slid onto her third finger as though it had been looking for a home. Paolo kissed her hand, turned it over and kissed her palm, then he kissed each fingertip.

'Come with me, Kirsty. I want to show you how much I adore you. I want—*Cristo*!' The pager, clipped to the other back pocket of Paolo's jeans, sounded a strident summons. Paolo threw up his hands, expansively outraged, and bounded down the steps. He opened the passenger door of the Porsche and snatched a cell phone from the seat.

'Tonolo,' he barked as soon as his call was answered. Kirsty pitied the poor registrar on the other end of the line. The cell phone was quickly discarded. Paolo looked thunderous.

'What have I done to deserve *this*?' he snarled. Then his expression became agonised. 'To be separated from the woman I love—on the night of our *fidanzamento*.'

Kirsty gulped. She had a fair idea what *fidanzamento* meant. How, precisely, had she allowed this to happen?

'Tomorrow, *cara*. Nothing will stop us. Don't forget!'

Forget! That was rather unlikely. Kirsty now held a small velvet box in each hand. The Porsche took off with a roar that sounded as frustrated as its owner. Kirsty turned, numbly, and let herself into the staff quarters. She ascended the three flights of steps very slowly. So slowly that she stopped and sat down halfway up the last flight.

What *had* she done? Kirsty took a very deep breath and held it for several heartbeats before releasing it cautiously. She knew exactly what she'd done. She, Kirsty McTavish, had just become engaged. Twice. To

two different men. On the same night. An approxima-
tion of a hollow laugh escaped her throat. She wasn't
dreaming. She had evidence that added up to a fright-
ening number of thousands of pounds. Kirsty set the
velvet box James had presented her with on the step
beside her. Then she eased the sapphire and diamond
creation off her finger and tucked it back into the slot
the silk lining of the other box provided. The box shut
with a decisive snap that seemed to echo around the
empty stairwell like the closing of a trap.

What, in God's name, was she going to do about
this?

Kirsty McTavish was not unused to getting herself
into scrapes but this one definitely took the biscuit.
First prize. The red rosette. The Academy Award for
creating chaos. The sound of a door shutting on the
second floor finally broke into the tumble of Kirsty's
thoughts. She glanced at her watch. One-thirty a.m!
How long had she been sitting here? How long had she
been standing outside, allowing Paolo to scramble her
brains with his passionate words and kisses? Kirsty got
to her feet a little unsteadily. This was one scrape she
was not going to be able to handle alone. She needed
help. Desperately.

There was no response to the tap on Ian Fraser's
door. Kirsty rapped more loudly.

'I'm not on call.' A muffled, very sleepy voice could
be heard.

Kirsty knocked again.

'I was on call last night.' The voice was less muffled.
'I will probably be on call *tomorrow* night.' Now it
sounded annoyed. And louder. 'But, tonight—I am
sleeping!' The door flew open. Ian stood there, wearing
nothing but a pair of silk boxer shorts. 'Kirsty!' he said

in astonishment. His gaze took in the sophisticated hairstyle, travelled down the length of the elegant black dress and landed on the high-heeled shoes before flicking back to her face. 'What on earth are you doing here? What's wrong this time?'

'I think I'm in trouble, Ian,' Kirsty said in a small voice. Ian's boxer shorts had on them a manic looking 'Roadrunner' with a cloud of dust behind him, a bubble enclosing the 'B-Beep!'

Ian pulled Kirsty in by the arm and shut the door quickly. He pushed her to a sitting position on the end of his rumpled bed.

'What do you mean—trouble? Are you pregnant?'

Kirsty laughed. 'Are you kidding? It would have to have been an immaculate conception.'

Ian didn't smile. 'You mean you're still a—'

'Don't *say* it!' Kirsty had both hands clenched into fists on her lap. Each fist enclosed a small velvet box. She uncurled one set of fingers. 'No. *This* is my problem.'

Ian reached for a T-shirt and pulled it on before taking the box. He flicked it open to stare at the square solitaire diamond ring.

'Very nice.' His face was expressionless. 'Am I supposed to congratulate you?'

'James gave it to me.' Kirsty was having trouble remembering precisely what she'd said to James. Or why she'd said it. 'It was a bit of a surprise. He's been so kind to me, Ian, and he's a very nice man. And I like his kids.'

'Good.' Ian didn't meet her eyes. He yawned with deliberation. 'I hope you'll all be very happy together. Now, can I get some sleep, please?'

'No.'

'Why not?'

'Because I've got a problem.'

'Seems to me you've just solved it. You'll be rich, famous and you won't even have to go through all the messy business of getting pregnant and having babies.'

'I *want* to get pregnant and have babies.'

'Well, don't tell me. That's not a problem I'm going to help you with. Talk to James.'

'Getting pregnant is not my problem, Ian.'

'Isn't it?' Ian's tone was waspish. 'Seems to me you're having a bit of trouble even losing your—'

'Don't *say* it!' Kirsty's eyes flashed. She extended her hand, palm up, exhibiting the other velvet box. '*This* is my problem.'

Ian stared at the box. He stared at Kirsty and then back at the box again. With a show of resigned willingness to humour her, he picked up the box and opened it.

'Very nice,' he said again. 'Do you get one for every other day of the week as well?'

'James didn't give me that one. Paolo did. Tonight.'

'Are you telling me you went out with James Fenwick *and* Paolo Tonolo tonight?' Ian gave a short burst of laughter. 'Is this like one of those movies where you have to keep saying you need to go to the loo and you rush from one table to the other to keep two dates happy?'

'No.' Kirsty shook her head. 'This isn't funny, Ian. I was standing outside after James brought me home and Paolo came along and started telling me he couldn't live without me and that Chantelle was history. And then he gave me this ring.'

'Which you accepted,' Ian said dryly.

'Kind of.' Kirsty sighed. 'It's a bit hard to explain.'

She bit her lip and gazed up at Ian desperately. 'What am I going to *do*, Ian?'

'You're asking *me*?' Ian turned away.

'Yes.' Kirsty was taken aback by the tension evident in Ian's tone and body posture. 'I thought you might help me.'

'Why?' Ian snapped. 'Why should I *want* to help you?'

Kirsty swallowed. 'We're friends. I thought...I thought you cared about me.'

'I do care about you,' Ian said angrily. 'I care about you far more than you could ever realise, or appreciate.' He rounded on Kirsty. 'You're naïve, Kirsty McTavish. You're childish and immature and you can't see past the surface of what anyone wants to offer you. You're shallow.' Ian's tone was bitter. 'You couldn't recognise true love—not the *genuine article*, if it tripped you up in the corridor.' Ian took two steps and flung his door open. 'I'm through with you, Kirsty. I don't want to pick up the pieces any more. You're too thick to even learn from experience. I've had enough. Go away and sort out your own bloody problems.'

Kirsty remained sitting on the end of the bed. Her vision was blurred by her tears and cleared only slightly when they began to roll down her cheeks. She could see a fuzzy image of Ian, snapping shut the jewellery cases. He slapped one into her right hand. Then he pushed the other into her left hand. Kirsty found herself being pulled roughly to her feet.

'Go away,' Ian said firmly. 'Choose by yourself. Throw a dice. Toss a coin. Play ''one potato, two potato''. I really don't care how you decide. I just don't want anything to do with it.' Kirsty was being propelled towards and through the door. 'And I don't want anything to do with *you*. Goodbye, Kirsty.'

Ian had never completed a circuit of Regent's Park so fast. His body seemed propelled by the same anger that had kept him awake for the rest of the night after Kirsty's visit. If he ran fast enough perhaps he could leave the anger—and the despair—behind him.

The strategy was partly successful. Most of the anger had gone by the time he donned his white coat and headed for Lizzie's cardiology ward. It wasn't Kirsty's fault. She wasn't really naïve. She was trusting and the trait was childish only in that most people had had it knocked out of them by the time they'd become adults. Kirsty was openly loving and ready to give more than others gave her. It was part of the reason Ian loved her so much. She attracted a warm emotional response from everybody and she wanted to give back everything she could. She was a prime target for the sophisticated approach that someone like James Fenwick or Paolo Tonolo could offer and she didn't want to believe that what they offered wasn't really good enough for her.

Perhaps it was. They could both offer maturity, wealth, glamour, a position in a society Ian had no desire even to enter. Ian couldn't compete. Not a chance. But what did they want from Kirsty? Paolo wanted her body, obviously. A virgin was probably an irresistible prize. But James Fenwick? Was he searching for a second chance of feeling young again—the classic resolution of a mid-life crisis? Or was he trying to provide his children with something missing in *their* lives.

Ian flicked though the case notes on Jane

Armstrong's desk. Oliver Reeves was due for his final intramuscular dose of antibiotics that would complete the ten day course they had initiated when his IV had been discontinued. He would be discharged, probably tomorrow, on a maintenance level of digoxin. The baby had done so well on medical management that there was no need to consider surgery at this time. They would follow him carefully and schedule a cardiac catheterisation test some time within the next three months.

It was quite likely that Oliver would not experience any further episodes of heart failure and that the hole in his heart would close spontaneously within the next couple of years. At least the finish of his antibiotic course would mean Ian wouldn't see Kirsty marching grimly through the ward with the syringe and swab in a kidney dish, looking as though she had been sent to dispatch a favourite cat. She hated being the one to inflict any painful procedures on children and Oliver had become understandably averse to needles during his stay in hospital.

Ian sighed heavily. So much for his resolution not to even *think* about Kirsty any more. Maybe he was wrong. Maybe all James Fenwick and Paolo wanted was to be loved by Kirsty. To be able to bask in the warmth her presence generated and to share the laughter that inevitably surrounded her. It was all Ian wanted, after all. Well, almost all. He couldn't deny how incredibly erotic he found her body. It was difficult to believe that either of the surgeons could feel as deeply about Kirsty as he did but what did that matter now? *He* hadn't produced a ring. He wasn't even in the running. Which one would she choose?

Ian flicked open another set of notes. Harry Wilton

was in for the day to have a series of tests including an exercise protocol on the treadmill. He could be lined up for another catheter test if any of the results were of concern. Ian decided to pay Harry a visit first, before he went off for the first scheduled test of an echocardiogram. Then he changed his mind. He could hear Harry singing as he neared Room Two. The tuneless accompaniment to the boy's enthusiastic warble could be coming from only one person. And he wanted to avoid the pain of seeing that person as much as possible.

'Where's Dr Bruce?' A frantic voice called.

Ian's head turned swiftly towards the entrance of the ward on the other side of Room One. The voice was coming from somewhere near the lifts.

'Help! I need some help!'

Kirsty emerged from Room Two at a run. She kept ahead of Ian as they both moved towards the cry for assistance. The woman was crouched over the still form of a child.

'It's Beth!' Kirsty cried in dismay. 'What's happened, Catherine?'

'She fainted—twice, on the way to school. We got a taxi and came straight here. Where's Dr Bruce?'

Ian had his hand on Beth's neck. 'She's got an arrhythmia—an abnormal heartbeat,' he told Catherine with concern. 'Did you not go to the emergency department?'

'No.' Catherine Wayland shook her head. 'They don't know Beth. I thought Dr Bruce would be able to see her…she needs help.'

'He's not here right now,' said Ian. 'But don't worry. We'll look after Beth.'

Jane Armstrong had joined them. 'I'll see that the

treatment room's clear,' she told Ian. 'Kirsty, you stay here.' Jane sped off.

'Has she been unwell at all in the last few days?' Ian had lifted the large child easily. She lay limply in his arms.

'No...well, she wet her bed last night. She hasn't done that for years.'

'You haven't altered the dose of her medications at all?' Ian was already moving towards the treatment room.

'No, I'm very careful. We use one of those special spoons with the hollow handles. Beth can't swallow pills.'

Ian nodded. He knew the size of Beth's tongue made swallowing tablets almost impossible. Jane was moving equipment in the treatment room.

'Let's get a monitor going,' Ian ordered. 'And make sure the defibrillator's charged.'

'Did you test that this morning, Kirsty?' Jane looked satisfied at Kirsty's nod. They were both removing Beth's clothing.

'Get a BP, thanks, Kirsty.' Ian was shining a torch into Beth's eyes. Jane began attaching sticky ECG electrodes.

'BP's eighty over forty-five,' Kirsty reported. 'I think.'

'You *think*?'

'There's lots of ectopic activity,' Kirsty said defensively. 'It's hard to know exactly when the sound disappears.'

Ian snorted unsympathetically. He watched as the interference cleared from the screen and the trace appeared. The rate was very slow, the complexes wide and there were frequent, abnormal ectopic beats.

'Forty-eight beats per minute,' he muttered. 'Way too slow.' He looked across at Beth's mother, standing anxiously at the foot of the bed. 'How wet was Beth's bed this morning?'

'Very wet. And she'd been to the toilet just before bedtime. She was desperate to go again as soon as she got up as well.'

'Did she eat or drink anything strange yesterday? Like dandelions?'

'No.' Catherine gave a fleeting smile. 'She does eat strange things occasionally but she's just got over a bit of a cold so she was staying inside.'

'Any other symptoms?'

'Yes. She had a sore tummy this morning and she said her eyes were funny. Everything looked yellow.'

Ian nodded. 'Let's get a blood sample off for a digoxin level and electrolytes, stat. I think she's got digoxin toxicity.'

Kirsty collected a syringe and vacutubes. Ian shook his head. 'Get a butterfly cannula, Kirsty,' he said impatiently. 'We need to get an IV line established.'

Kirsty swapped the syringe for an IV-giving set and gave Ian an apologetic glance. He looked away.

'See if you can get hold of Charles, Jane, and let him know what's happening.' Ian taped down the butterfly cannula and attached a syringe to draw blood. 'Kirsty, get an IV set up and then get me some lignocaine. One mg per kg bolus and we'll add some more to the IV solution. I also want Dilantin, five mg per kg.' An alarm sounding on the cardiac monitor caught Ian's attention. 'Set up a pacemaker trolley as well.' Kirsty was looking from one corner of the room to the other, scanning the supply shelves. *'Now!'* barked Ian.

Jane Armstrong reappeared as Beth's heart-rate

dropped to dangerous levels. She led Beth's mother out of the room quickly. Charles Bruce entered hurriedly as Kirsty was handing Ian the first of the drugs he had ordered, holding up the empty vial as well so that he could double-check the dosage. Jane was right behind Charles.

'Looks like dig toxicity,' Ian told his consultant. 'I've started her on lignocaine and given her Dilantin. She's been unconscious since she came in.'

Charles was watching the ECG screen. 'We're going to need to pace her. I'll get scrubbed.'

Kirsty was busy scribbling on the blood-sample test-tubes.

'Get a move on, Kirsty,' Ian ordered sharply. 'We need those results, *now!*'

Kirsty got a move on. She was glad of an excuse to escape. Jade Reynolds' tamponade had been just as much of an emergency as Beth's condition presently was but she and Ian had managed as a fluid team then. Now she couldn't do anything to the registrar's satisfaction.

Kirsty had spent the rest of last night totally stunned by Ian's shredding of her personality. He obviously meant it. She was too immature and 'thick' to warrant any further attention from Ian Fraser. He wanted nothing more to do with her. Somehow, the realisation that he intended to carry through the abandonment of their friendship was more significant than the other problem Kirsty now faced.

The problem of her double engagement.

Chapter Eight

'POTASSIUM level's sky-high.'

'Digoxin level's up to eight.' Ian whistled in disbelief. Therapeutic levels were kept between one and three. 'She must have overdosed on digoxin somehow. The diuresis isn't enough to explain this.'

'Have you ordered the digoxin-specific antibodies?' Charles Bruce was watching the monitor screen above Beth Wayland's bed.

'They're running IV now.'

'Good.' Charles nodded. 'That should get the digoxin and potassium levels down within the next few hours.'

'We'll need to find out how she managed to get an overdose. Her mother has no idea.'

'Has she shown any signs of regaining consciousness?'

'Just. She's not making much sense yet.'

'I wonder if we should get her up to Intensive Care. She's going to need constant monitoring while we've got this pacing wire in.'

'Her mother was very keen to get her in here under your care. Beth's not too good with total strangers and Catherine's had a pretty big fright.'

Charles Bruce took a final glance at the monitor. 'Pacing's going well. She's got a good rate and her blood pressure's up. I guess we can keep her here for the moment. Do another dig level and electrolytes in a couple of hours. If we're not getting on top of it we'll transfer her. Make sure the defibrillator's charged up and that someone's with her at all times.'

Kirsty came back into the room with Catherine Wayland who was carrying a small suitcase.

'My neighbour just brought in a few of Beth's things,' Catherine explained to the doctors. 'I'm so glad you're here, Dr Bruce. How is she?'

'We've got things under control but we're going to have to watch her rather carefully for a while. We're pretty sure she's managed an overdose of her digoxin and possibly the frusemide as well.'

Catherine nodded. 'I got my neighbour to bring the bottles in, like you asked. The level's well down on both of them. I can't understand it—I'm so careful!'

'Could she have taken it by herself?'

'No. She hates taking medicine. I have to bribe her with sweets. If she was going to help herself to anything, it would be the sweets, not the medicine.'

'Perhaps she can tell us when she wakes up properly.' Charles glanced at Kirsty, who had helped unpack Beth's clothes and toys and was now heading for the door. 'Are you going somewhere, Kirsty?'

'Yes, Dr Bruce. I have to take Harry for his exercise test.'

'Ask Jane to get someone to come in here, then. Beth needs constant observation. Ian's going to keep an eye on her here instead of shifting her to Intensive Care.'

'Oh, good!' Catherine breathed a sigh of relief. 'I feel so much better having her here with the people she knows.'

Kirsty nodded and left the room. She would pass the message on to Jane but she would also do her best to ensure that she wasn't chosen for the duty. The few minutes she had been in Beth's room were enough to reveal that Ian was trying to ignore her. He hadn't even made eye contact, seemingly absorbed in Beth's chart while Charles had been talking to Catherine. To have to spend hours in the child's room waiting for frequent visits by someone who clearly wanted nothing to do with her would be more than Kirsty could take right now.

Two minutes later Kirsty wished she *had* stayed in Beth's room. The surgical team had been to visit Harry Wilton to review the results of the echo and the chest X-ray and to discuss the exercise test. Both men had smiled at Kirsty in a very welcoming manner. The gaze of both men had gone to her left hand. She could almost see a bubble over their heads containing an engagement ring. *Two* engagement rings. Kirsty put her hands behind her back and smiled guiltily. James Fenwick and Paolo both looked understanding and then they caught each other's gaze and Kirsty was aware of a peculiar stillness. A kind of crackle in the atmosphere. Her hands felt distinctly damp. She wiped them surreptitiously on the back of her black trousers and desperately tried to think of some reason to plausibly excuse herself from the room.

James asked Paolo to chase up Harry's X-ray film from the office.

'I could do that,' Kirsty offered eagerly.

'You could come with me,' Paolo suggested. His eyes suggested that they could bypass the office and find the nearest available linen closet.

'No.' James Fenwick's tone was sharp. 'I want to discuss the timetable for the rest of Harry's investigations with Nurse McTavish.'

Harry had picked up his latest 'Goosebumps' book

and was totally absorbed. James stepped over to Kirsty as soon as Paolo left the room.

'Dinner, tonight. I'll pick you up at seven.'

It wasn't an invitation. James was simply stating a fact. Very warmly. Kirsty wanted to refuse but she had no opportunity. Paolo had made the trip to the office and back in record time. He gave Kirsty a brilliant smile. James Fenwick glowered at his registrar as he took the X-ray film. He snapped it under the clip on the viewing screen and studied it briefly, giving a satisfied nod.

'Right, that's fine. We'll see you later, Harry.'

Harry glanced up from his book and nodded. James turned to his registrar. 'Who's next?'

'David Martin. Yesterday's VSD repair. He's still in the ICU.'

'Let's go, then.' James gave Kirsty a purely professional nod. Paolo blew her a kiss as soon as his consultant's back was turned. Kirsty breathed a sigh of relief but the reprieve was only brief. Thirty seconds later Paolo popped back into Harry's room just as Kirsty was finding a dressing gown for Harry to wear.

'I forgot to return the X-ray.' Paolo pulled it from the screen with a look that led Kirsty to believe the omission had been quite deliberate. He lowered his voice urgently as he stepped closer to Kirsty.

'Kirsty—*cara*! Why are you not wearing your ring?'

Which one? Kirsty thought wildly. She gave a hollow laugh. 'I couldn't wear it to work, Paolo. It's far too big.'

'Yes.' Paolo nodded happily. 'But anything smaller could not have expressed how I feel about you.'

Harry looked up with interest. 'Can I see your ring?'

'No!' Kirsty's tone was far sharper than she'd intended. 'Sorry, Harry. I left it at home.'

'What does it look like?'

Kirsty turned to Paolo. 'You'd better go, Paolo. We can't talk about this here.'

Paolo sighed. 'Tonight, then. I will come and get you. Six-thirty p.m.'

'No!—I can't,' Kirsty stammered.

'Why not, *cara*?' Paolo lowered his voice even more. 'I need to be with you.'

'I can't. I've got something on at seven p.m.'

'Not something as important as *us*, surely?'

Kirsty's thoughts raced in desperation. Could she plead prior knowledge of a migraine that was due to hit at five p.m? A split shift so that she would still be on duty?

'It's…ah…a group thing,' Kirsty invented. 'I can't let everybody down. We're…ah…' inspiration struck '…we're helping each other get our costumes ready for the Halloween Ball. A kind of dress rehearsal.'

'Ah…the Halloween Ball.' Paolo was staring intently at Kirsty. 'What a wonderful occasion for a public announcement. Then everyone will know.'

'Everyone,' Kirsty echoed. The ball was tomorrow. Could that possibly be enough time to sort out the mess she was in? Paolo's beep sounded.

'James is wondering where I am,' he said tolerantly. He leaned forward and placed a lingering kiss on Kirsty's lips.

'Wow!' Harry crowed. His book was forgotten.

'Just as well James is not here,' Paolo murmured. He gave Kirsty another brief kiss in parting.

'Just as well,' Kirsty agreed. Harry's dressing gown

was hanging limply from her fingers even after Paolo had gone.

'Wow!' Harry repeated. 'He really likes you, doesn't he, Kirsty?'

'Mmm.' Kirsty was having trouble focusing on the task of getting Harry ready to move.

'Has he heard you singing, yet?'

The table was at the same restaurant. In fact, it was the same table. Kirsty tried to fight the wave of *déjà vu*.

She was even wearing the same black dress. Well, there hadn't been much of a choice there. It had been either the black dress, the brown suit or the witch's costume from the hire shop now sitting in the corner of her bedroom. And James was wearing the same evening suit he had worn the night before. He ordered the same dinner.

Kirsty couldn't help herself. 'But you had that last night,' she exclaimed.

'I eat here quite frequently. I know what I like.'

'So you always have the same thing?'

'Usually.'

'At the same table?'

'If it's available.' James Fenwick's slightly smug expression suggested that the availability wasn't often a problem.

'Just different women, then?' Kirsty was smiling.

'Pardon?' James did not appear amused.

'Oh, nothing.' Kirsty eyed the stony-faced waiter. 'I'll have the usual, too, thanks.'

'Excuse me?'

Kirsty sighed. Her humour was not going down well. She reordered, pointing rapidly at the menu, making sure that her choice was completely different from her last meal here. Then she waited while James had a lengthy discussion and wine-tasting session with the wine steward. When her glass was finally filled, Kirsty took a grateful—and rather large—swallow.

'I thought we could use a little time to talk.' James sipped his wine and set the glass down again carefully. 'To get to know each other a little better.'

Kirsty took another swallow of her wine. Why did he want to marry her, she wondered, when he really didn't know her at all?

'OK,' she agreed. 'What shall we talk about?'

'Travel?' suggested James.

'Oh, I love travel.' Kirsty nodded. 'At least, I'm sure I will once I get the opportunity.'

'You will have any number of opportunities when we're married. Or perhaps I *should* say "if".' His smile was a repeat of the table-availability confidence.

'Perhaps,' Kirsty echoed. 'Is it mostly conferences you travel to, James?'

'Yes, but don't worry. Almost all international conferences have a full programme for partners. Bus excursions, sightseeing, shopping. The usual things the wives enjoy.'

'Oh.' Kirsty could imagine a busload of surgeons' wives, fingering foreign goods and flashing gold credit cards. They'd all be old, probably fat and definitely overdressed. 'Any cruises?' she asked hopefully. Paolo's family yacht was massive. They toured all over the Mediterranean on regular holidays, by all accounts. Sand and sun and no stuffy buses.

'I'll keep an eye out,' James promised as their entrées arrived.

Kirsty was trying smoked salmon for the first time. It tasted raw. She poked it around with her fork and had a sudden vision of a pair of roller blades landing on her plate. She disguised her giggle as a cough and reached apologetically for her wineglass.

'Water might be more effective,' James suggested mildly.

'I like wine,' Kirsty responded firmly. She had the feeling that she and James Fenwick were patently not on the same wavelength. She felt the sophistication that the surgeon had inspired in her evaporating and Kirsty had to work hard not to give in to the temptation to misbehave. It must be the restaurant, she decided. Too rigid, no scope for the imagination. Like working in theatre. No wonder James approved. Ian would hate it.

Kirsty toyed with her salmon. No bus tours and shopping binges would go with travelling with Ian. And no luxury yachts. More likely a Eurorail pass and backpacks. And much more likely to be an exciting adventure.

'You don't like your smoked salmon?' James was looking concerned.

'No,' Kirsty said. Maybe it was time for a little honesty. 'Sorry, but I think it's revolting.'

'No problem.' James merely looked up and a waiter glided towards them.

'Is he wearing roller blades?' Kirsty asked.

James appeared not to have heard. 'I'm taking the children down to our country house in the weekend,' he said calmly. 'Perhaps you'd like to join us?'

'Your country house?' Kirsty evaded responding to the invitation.

'It's in Surrey. Not too far. We also have a villa in Tuscany for the holidays.'

'Paolo's family has a castle in Tuscany,' Kirsty offered. 'Is it nearby?'

'I hope I'm not competing with Paolo Tonolo, here, Kirsty.'

'Um…no, of course not.'

'I know you *were* seeing him.'

'I haven't been out with him for weeks,' Kirsty said truthfully.

'So how exactly do things stand between the two of you?' James Fenwick's gaze was sharp enough to cut herself on.

'Um…a wee bit tricky,' Kirsty answered, also truthfully. She crossed her fingers. 'I'll sort it out.'

'Good.' James was distracted by the arrival of their main course. They were silent for some time and Kirsty cautiously attacked the dish she'd ordered so hurriedly. She hadn't been going to admit she couldn't understand the French and she hadn't taken the time to even glance at the description. Were those truffles or *snails*?

'So you'd be happy to hand in your resignation?'

'Sorry?' Kirsty's attention snapped back.

'At St Elizabeth's. It really wouldn't be very practical to have you nursing there when we're…*if* we're—'

'Oh, I couldn't give up nursing,' Kirsty interrupted. 'I *love* my job.'

James regarded her steadily. 'Well, perhaps some part-time employment somewhere privately, then. I'll see what I can arrange.'

'No, don't—please!' Kirsty felt as if the room were getting smaller. She reached for her water glass but picked up the wine by mistake. 'I couldn't *not* work,' she said earnestly. 'What on earth would I do?'

'You'll want to be available to travel to conferences with me and of course you'll have a very full social life. You'll be pleased to know that I always get a full season ticket to Glyndebourne.'

'Oh.' The room got smaller again. 'You really like opera, then?'

'Of course. Don't you? You appeared to be enjoying it when I saw you there with young Tonolo.'

Young! He was eleven years older than Kirsty!

'Actually,' Kirsty said, 'I prefer rock and roll. And the sort of music you're always telling Sarah to turn down, or else!'

James Fenwick's smile was tolerant. 'Opera *is* an acquired taste.'

'Like snails,' Kirsty said mournfully. The pile of shrivelled black objects at the side of her plate had grown considerably.

A silence descended as their plates were removed. James didn't break it until the desserts arrived.

'Is there anything else you'd like to talk about, Kirsty?'

'Yes.' Kirsty gave James a very direct look. 'How do you feel about children?'

'I'm very fond of them. Especially my own.'

'Yes, I know.' Kirsty smiled. The tolerance and affection James had towards his children was one of the things she liked most about him. 'What I meant was, how do feel about *more* children?'

James looked taken aback. Very taken aback. 'I hadn't given it any consideration,' he admitted. 'In fact, it may not even be possible. It's a long time since I had…ah…'

'A trip to the vet?' Kirsty offered.

James laughed. 'Quite.' He was still laughing as he gazed at Kirsty. 'I do love your sense of humour,' he said finally.

'Thanks.' Kirsty subsided into silence again. James obviously didn't want more children. Paolo, on the other hand, wanted 'many beautiful babies'. A genuine but casual desire, like ordering extra fries at McDonald's. And Ian? Ian had never talked about the desire to have children but his love for them was evident every day. Ian would be a wonderful father. She could picture a baby with flaming red curly hair, sitting in a cot and shrieking with glee at the furry black spider jumping nearby.

'You're not listening to me, Kirsty,' James chided gently.

'I'm not? Sorry.'

'I was asking whether you had any decorating preferences. I have a team of interior designers looking at the house next week.'

'Which house?'

'The Knightsbridge address, of course. You haven't seen the others so I'd hardly expect you to have formed an opinion about them.'

'Your house is fine,' Kirsty said quietly. 'It doesn't need anything done.' What could you give a house that already had everything? Paolo would have the same problem. An expensive tweak to the colour scheme maybe to sustain a little interest in the surroundings. England or Italy. Kirsty imagined that the lifestyle of the extremely wealthy would be similar everywhere. And New Zealand? Ian was apparently planning to return to his home town of Dunedin. 'Little Edinburgh.' He'd probably buy some damp little stone cottage reminiscent of Scotland. It would rain all the time and they'd never be able to afford central heating.

They'd have to have open fires. Roaring log fires with a comfortable hearthrug and their favourite music and a glass of wine once that red-haired baby was finally asleep...Kirsty blinked hard. Why did she feel so much like crying all of a sudden?

'Kirsty?' The query was sharp. 'What's the matter?'

Kirsty took a deep breath. 'I can't possibly marry you, James. I'm sorry.'

'You don't need to give me your answer right now, Kirsty. I'm not putting you under any pressure, I hope.'

'I really like you, James. And I really like Sarah and George and I'm sorry if they'll be disappointed but I can't marry you.' Kirsty's words tumbled out. 'It would never work.'

'Why is that?'

'I get drunk sometimes.' Why on earth had she confessed to that? Kirsty knew why. She knew that Ian would care for her no matter what. He had already proved it. 'I throw up all over the place,' Kirsty added for good measure. 'It's quite horrible.'

'I'm sure it is.' James Fenwick didn't look disgusted. He looked...amused. Like a parent discussing the reprehensible behaviour of an adored child. 'I hope it won't happen *too* often.'

Kirsty looked away. 'That's not the only reason why I can't marry you, James.'

'What are the other reasons, Kirsty?' James asked quietly. He was listening, his smile fading, but there was no anger in his expression. He looked more resigned than anything else.

Kirsty spoke seriously. 'I'm too young for you, James.'

'You mean I'm too old for *you*.'

'No. I'm talking about experience. Life.' Kirsty fiddled with the stem of her wineglass. James waited silently for her to continue. 'My mother always made me save up for anything I wanted when I was little. She said I would never appreciate things unless I earned them.'

'So money's the problem?'

'Not exactly. You've already done the things I need to do. Like getting to know foreign cities by using public transport. Like choosing the first house you buy and saving up for furniture. Like having a baby and watching it grow up.'

'You could have a baby if it's that important to you, Kirsty. Reversals can be effective.'

'No.' Kirsty shook her head. 'My baby needs to have a father that wants it as much as I do.'

'Sarah and George will be sorry. They miss their mother.'

'I could never replace their mother.' Kirsty was horrified at the thought. 'I'd be a hopeless stepmother, too. The children would be more like siblings to me.'

'Think about it just a little more,' James urged. 'I would be very sorry myself to lose your company. I have a lot to offer you,' he added wistfully.

'I know,' Kirsty said sadly. 'And there are probably a lot of women who'd give their eye-teeth to accept. But I can't. I'm sorry, James.'

The silence was tense. Then James smiled. 'I don't really fancy a woman with no eye-teeth.'

Kirsty laughed, grateful to feel more at ease. James was accepting her refusal. He wasn't angry. She had been right—James Fenwick was a very nice man.

'Shall we go?'

The car was waiting at the front door. James glanced at Kirsty as they cleared the first set of traffic lights.

'I would have been branded a cradle-snatcher, of course. There are those who have been in contact with

Sir Brian who already believe I'm having some sort of a mid-life crisis.'

Kirsty laughed obligingly and tried not to think of what Ian's reaction to the confession would have been.

'I would have been quite prepared to tolerate the innuendo but it would have been very unfair on you.' James was silent for a minute. 'If nothing else, you've shown me how to relate to my own children. I have to thank you for that, Kirsty.'

He pulled the Daimler to a smooth halt outside the staff quarters. Kirsty cleared her throat nervously.

'I'll put the ring in your office tomorrow.'

'You're welcome to keep it, Kirsty.'

'I couldn't possibly do that!' Kirsty's eyes were round with horror. James laughed.

'You're a very special young woman, Kirsty McTavish. I hope the man you do choose will realise how lucky he is.'

Kirsty smiled. 'Thanks, James. And not just for the compliment. You've helped me grow up a little, I think. Made me think about things. I understand a lot more about what I want out of life.'

'I hope you find it, Kirsty.'

'Oh, I think I will. I think I might even know where it is.'

The sound of Ian's chanter could be heard from the top of the stairs. Kirsty went past her own door and kept going, drawn by the sound. She stood outside Ian's door. He was playing 'Amazing Grace'. Kirsty tapped tentatively on the door. She wasn't sure what she was going to say. Perhaps there would be no need to say anything. Ian understood her. If she was feeling this strongly then he should be able to take one look at her and know how much she loved him. She wouldn't have to admit to her misguided chasing after some romantic fantasy to explain her stupid behaviour. They could wipe the slate clean and start again.

Not right at the beginning. Maybe just before that visit to Glyndebourne so that Kirsty would not have been intoxicated by Paolo's physical expertise. So that when they'd gone for that swim and Ian had kissed her she would have recognised that passion *could* grow from friendship. That, in fact, their friendship had just been laying the foundation stones for a lifetime of love and companionship. *And* passion.

Kirsty's knock went unanswered. Unheard. She considered knocking more loudly but her hand slowly dropped to her side. Ian had told her he'd had enough of her. That he wanted nothing more to do with her. He had every right to feel angry. She hadn't just rejected him in favour of another man. She had rejected him in favour of *two* other men, one of whom was still theoretically in the picture.

How would she feel if she thought she was number three on the list but Ian had finally decided it was worth giving her a whirl? Not very impressed, she decided. She would probably tell him to get lost. Unless…unless she loved him very much.

Kirsty's hand crept up again. The sound of the chanter ceased abruptly. She could hear Ian moving around his room. Suddenly the door opened and Ian was standing in front of her, an empty coffee mug from the kitchen in his hand. His astonished expression quickly hardened.

'Something I can do for you, Kirsty?' he asked with chilling courtesy.

'I…um…I liked the music.' Kirsty's voice had a distinct wobble. 'You're getting better.'

'Some things in life are *worth* persevering with.'

Kirsty felt a wave of despair. The message was clear. His relationship with her was *not* one of the things worth persevering with. It was finished. Kirsty couldn't say anything. Words and emotions raced through her head, colliding with each other and preventing anything coherent rising far enough to the surface to be expressed. The silence was agonising. There was too much Kirsty wanted to say and no way in the world she could say anything. She turned and moved woodenly towards the sanctuary of her own room.

Kirsty felt curiously calm by the time she got there. She didn't want to cry. Her feeling ran too deep for that. Emotions and thoughts she had never felt before vied for prominence. Kirsty's emotional horizons had expanded tonight. She understood what really counted in life. Ian would have approved. Kirsty could recognise the genuine article. And it had been taken out of reach.

Two small velvet boxes were sitting in the top drawer of Kirsty's bedside table. She removed them and flipped them open. She hadn't loved either of the men who had given her these extravagant tokens. The gratitude and respect she felt for James Fenwick and the appeal of being part of a family had confused her. The physical excitement Paolo had awakened in her had confused her even more. The emotions had been powerful. Powerful enough to make her think that was all there was to it. Now she knew the truth. Kirsty felt immeasurably older and wiser.

Still calm, she reached for the telephone and dialled Paolo's number. Carlos seemed reluctant to transfer the call to his master's room.

'It's an emergency,' Kirsty told him firmly.

The phone rang. And rang. Finally it was picked up.
'Allo?'

A female voice. A French accent. Kirsty almost smiled. 'That's not Chantelle, is it?' she asked pleasantly.

'Oui, chérie. Who is this, please?'

Nobody for you to worry about, Kirsty thought. She didn't have the chance to say anything. She listened, intrigued. Chantelle could even shriek and giggle with a French accent. The sound of the phone being dropped made Kirsty wince but she kept listening.

'No! No, Paolo! Stop! I am cold. I have to get some clothes on.'

A deeper rumble of a male voice. Another giggle. Then the phone was picked up.

'Hello?' It was Paolo. 'Is anyone there?'

'Hi, Paolo,' Kirsty said brightly.

There was a long silence. Kirsty enjoyed it. This was a lot easier than she had anticipated. She felt in control for the first time in...the first time ever, probably.

'Are you still there, Paolo?'

'Sì. I...I don't know what to say, *cara.'*

'I do,' Kirsty assured him. 'Our relationship is over, Paolo. In fact, it never really existed at all. I'll put the ring in your office tomorrow.'

'No! I can explain everything.'

'I know,' Kirsty agreed kindly. 'Chantelle is history. Go back to bed, Paolo. You're probably getting cold as well.'

Kirsty put the phone down. She picked up the box containing Paolo's ring and snapped it shut. Then she repeated her actions with James Fenwick's ring. They sounded like miniature doors slamming.

'Back to square one,' Kirsty muttered wryly. 'And I'm *still* a virgin!'

Chapter Nine

THE baby was utterly miserable.

The eight-month-old baby sat in his cot, his red face at odds with the carrot-coloured fluff on top of his head. Felix was not a pretty baby and he was not crying loudly enough to attract the attention of nearby nursing staff. The grim downward turn of his mouth had given his chin deep dimples and his eyes were narrowed into exhausted slits but Felix was not giving up. His sobs were just loud hiccups but it was the lone tear that rolled over a red cheek that was Ian's undoing.

He leaned over the cot and undid the waist restraint that confined the remarkably mobile infant. Felix's arms shot up over his head, a desperate, mute appeal to be picked up. Ian complied.

'I know just how you feel, wee man,' he whispered. 'Life's a bitch sometimes, isn't it?'

As it had been last night when Ian had turned away from the equally desperate, mute appeal in Kirsty McTavish's expression. It would have been so easy to have responded. To have patted Kirsty on the back and told her that everything would be all right. That *he* was there for her and always would be. That he knew what she really wanted, had known all along even when she had had no idea, and that it was exactly what he wanted himself.

But that would have resolved nothing. Unless Kirsty came to the realisation unaided then Ian would never be sure that she really did understand. That she was sure, in her own heart, about what really mattered. And he wasn't going to make it too easy for her. If their relationship meant as much to her as it did to him, then any amount of difficulty would be tackled—and overcome.

He'd tried to give Kirsty a hint last night, telling her that some things in life were *worth* persevering with. He'd wanted her to agree. 'Like us,' he'd almost added, but Kirsty had already turned away, unwilling to tackle even the first obstacle of his deliberate coolness.

Ian sat down at Jane Armstrong's desk, Felix still in his arms. The baby had relaxed and the snuffling dampness against Ian's neck suggested that he was going to sleep. Ian opened a set of case notes, supporting Felix with one arm as he began to make notes about his earlier examination of Beth Wayland.

The digoxin-specific antibodies had done their job well. Beth's potassium and digoxin levels had fallen by thirty per cent over several hours and her heartbeat had reverted to a normal sinus rhythm with a rate of ninety beats per minute. She was going to need continued monitoring and treatment until the digoxin levels were well under toxic range which could take a week or longer. They also needed to find out how Beth had managed to get the overdose.

Beth had denied taking anything herself but her stubborn silence on further questioning suggested another story. There was no point pushing it. When Beth's stubborn streak was activated it was an impenetrable forcefield, as Catherine well knew.

'Just ignore it,' she'd advised Ian. 'In an hour or so she will have forgotten what it was about and she'll be all smiles and cooperation again.'

Kirsty stood in the office doorway silently. Ian

hadn't seen her. He was absorbed in his writing. The baby in his arms was sound asleep, his cheek flattened against Ian's shoulder, the pressure pushing his mouth open into a wide, squashed pout. One fat little arm dangled limply over Ian's bicep. Felix looked as though he'd been searching for exactly this place to finally feel safe enough to give in to his exhaustion. Poor baby. His mother had declared a total aversion to hospitals and hadn't even been in to visit during the two days of his admission so far.

Ian's head tilted slightly so that his own cheek rested against the baby's head. Kirsty's heart gave a painful thump. He would look just like that if he were holding his own baby. Felix even had red hair! As if to bury the poignant impression even deeper, Ian turned and brushed his lips against the baby's fluffy head in a soft kiss. Then his gaze flicked up, startled, as he caught sight of Kirsty. He shifted, seeming ill at ease to be under her quiet scrutiny. Was it her unwelcome presence or the fact that someone had witnessed what he'd probably thought was a private, tender moment?

'It's time for Felix to have his medication,' Kirsty said apologetically. 'Though he looks so happy I hate to disturb him.'

Ian was on his feet quickly. 'I have to go, anyway. I've been roped into the gang decorating the gymnasium for the Halloween Ball.'

'Oh, of course. It's tonight. I'd almost forgotten about it.' The thought of dressing up and having a good time was a long way away from Kirsty's present inclinations. 'I'm not sure I'll go, after all.' Would Ian be bothered by that? They'd planned to go together—a long time ago.

'That's a shame,' Ian said blandly. 'Wouldn't miss

it, myself. It should be a great night.' He carefully handed the sleeping baby over to Kirsty but Felix woke as she took hold of him. The baby looked up at Kirsty's face and his own puckered menacingly. He gave his first experimental wail as someone else entered the office.

'Heidi!' Ian sounded delighted. 'Haven't seen you for days.'

'I'm on leave.' The echo technician was wearing blue jeans and an embroidered peasant-style blouse. Kirsty jiggled Felix, trying to soothe him as she smiled a greeting at Heidi.

'Hope you're having a good break. What brings you in here?'

'Ian.' Heidi smiled back.

Kirsty's smile faded rapidly. Why not? Heidi was very attractive—especially out of uniform and with her pale blonde hair falling loosely around her shoulders. She was also petite, demure, well behaved at all times—all the things Kirsty could never be. Heidi would never get engaged to two different men on the same night. Heidi would never get drunk. Heidi could probably sing like an angel. A *blonde* angel.

'I'm helping do up the gym for tonight,' Heidi said, happily unaware of the resentment boiling in Kirsty. 'Someone said Ian was coming to help and I needed a break from blowing up balloons. There's something a bit weird about black balloons, don't you think?'

'How's it going?' Ian's face was animated.

'Great. Do you think Jane would let us borrow some sheets? Someone has sneaked a tank of helium out of the respiratory department. We were going to get balloons floating by themselves and drape sheets over them to make—'

'Ghosts!' Ian finished for her. 'Brilliant. Let's go and ask Jane. I was just on my way down.' He grimaced as Felix achieved a new level of decibels. 'I could do with a break.'

'I hear you're planning a rather long break.' Heidi waited by the door for Ian. 'Is it true you're heading back to New Zealand when you've finished your run on Cardiology?'

Ian's affirmation was quiet but decisive. He didn't look at Kirsty. 'In three weeks,' he added. ' I'm ready to go home, I think.'

Kirsty's hold on Felix tightened. Ian hadn't talked to her about leaving Lizzie's. He really had given up on her. Now he was planning to disappear completely from her life. The unhappy wailing of the baby in her arms underlined Kirsty's own feeling of desolation as she carried Felix back to his room. Ian and Heidi walked past the door a moment later. Jane Armstrong was right behind them.

'Don't tell anybody where those sheets came from. And make *sure* they get back here tomorrow. Undamaged!'

Ian and Heidi both laughed. Kirsty turned back to her task of changing a very dirty nappy. She hadn't heard Ian laugh for ages. *She* hadn't laughed for ages. Kirsty sighed deeply as she stuck down the fastening of Felix's clean nappy. She wanted life to return to what it had been all those weeks ago before she had set out to become something that she wasn't. She had thought she was growing up. Dressing elegantly, learning a bit of sophistication, stopping singing…letting herself believe she could be as gorgeous and desirable as Paolo's eyes had invited her to.

'I just want to be *me*,' Kirsty whispered to Felix as

she picked him up again. 'And there's only one person that ever loved me just for that.'

Kirsty moved quietly around the ward trying to avoid conversations that all seemed centred on the excitement of the ball. Jane Armstrong was looking steadily grumpier.

'Goodness knows what state those sheets will come back in.' She clicked her tongue. 'And *another* junior has rung in sick for the late shift. I wonder just how sick she really is.'

'I could stay on if you like,' Kirsty offered. 'I'm not that fussed about going to the ball.'

'Really?' Jane gave Kirsty a puzzled glance. 'I thought you and…' The charge nurse clearly decided against voicing her thought. 'If you could stay on that would be wonderful. Just till nine p.m. so you could help cover the drug round and getting everyone settled.'

Kirsty nodded. What had Jane been going to say? That she thought Kirsty would be attending the ball with Paolo? Or had she caught some gossip about James Fenwick? No wonder she had opted out of opening that potential can of worms. Kirsty thought of the small velvet boxes she had left on the desks of both the surgeons early that morning. She had sorted out the problem. So why did she feel more miserable than ever?

Returning a wheelchair to the A and E department a little later, Kirsty could feel the buzz of excitement running right through Lizzie's. She spotted Heidi and a nurse pushing a trolley covered with large artificial pumpkins. The faces cut into the pumpkins all seemed to be staring and grinning at Kirsty as the trolley came closer.

'These are for the tables,' Heidi told her. 'They have candles inside. Aren't they great?'

Kirsty nodded. 'How's it all going?' she asked politely.

'It's such fun!' Heidi exclaimed. 'Ian's been breathing the helium for the balloons and talking like Donald Duck. It's a scream!'

'I'll bet.' Kirsty's smile felt pasted into place.

'He won't tell anyone what his costume is. Do you know, Kirsty?'

Kirsty shrugged. 'Maybe he wants it to be a surprise.'

'We'll find out. We're all going to meet up at the pub first. What are you coming as, Kirsty?'

'I'm working.'

'Oh, poor you!' Heidi and her companion both looked sympathetic. 'I guess somebody has to. We're going as ghosts. We've got yards of plastic chain to rattle.'

Kirsty gave her wheelchair a firm shove. 'Have fun.' She walked away rapidly. There was a whole day of this to get through. She would just have to keep as busy as possible.

Back on the ward, Kirsty helped Harry Wilton pack his bag to go home. He had been kept in overnight to rest after the series of tests but the results had been excellent and Harry was excited. He had been sharing his room with Beth Wayland again but Beth looked less than cheerful when Harry bid her an enthusiastic farewell. As soon as Kirsty had seen Harry and his parents into the lift, she hurried back.

'What's up, Beth? Are you feeling sick again?'

'I only wanted to get better.'

'You are getting better, darling. You'll be able to go home again in a few days.'

'Medicine makes me better. That's what Mummy said.'

Kirsty nodded. 'That's why you need to stay with us for a wee while. So we can decide what the best medicine is. Did seeing Harry go home make you sad, Beth? Do you want to go home now?'

Beth folded her arms, a stubborn expression settling on her face. Kirsty realised she wasn't understanding what Beth was trying to say. She sat down on the side of the bed and put her arm around Beth. She sat quietly, having given the girl an encouraging squeeze.

'That's why I took *all* my medicine.'

'So you would get better faster?'

Beth nodded. 'I wanted Mummy to smile.'

'But it made you sick, didn't it?' Kirsty said gently.

'It made Mummy cry. And she'll be cross if I tell her.'

'No, she won't,' Kirsty promised. 'You won't do it again, will you, Beth?'

Beth shook her head slowly. Then she unfolded her arms and smiled at Kirsty. 'Can we play another trick on Dr Ian?'

Kirsty shook her head. She'd played more than enough tricks on 'Dr Ian'. 'He's not here at the moment, Beth. He's helping the other doctors get ready for a big party.'

'Can I come?'

'No, it's just for grown-ups, I'm afraid.'

'But I want Dr Ian.' Beth's arms folded again.

So do I, Beth, Kirsty thought unhappily. So do I.

*   *   *

The afternoon and evening crawled by. Kirsty only saw Ian once more, just before he left for the day.

'Better go,' he announced cheerfully. 'I've got to get the glue to stick those bolts on my neck.'

So he *was* going as Frankenstein. The reminder of the good-humoured banter they had shared was another twist of the knife for Kirsty. If only she could turn the clock back. Learning from experience was all very well but it wasn't much of a comfort when the price paid was so high.

By nine p.m. Kirsty was glad to leave the ward. It had been a long and miserable day. Sitting alone in her room in a deserted staff quarters was no improvement, however. Kirsty was reminded of the night of her mother's funeral. Sitting alone and wondering where her life was going and what she wanted to get out of it. Now she knew exactly what she wanted out of it.

Maybe the plot hadn't run as smoothly as one of her mother's favourite stories and maybe the hero wasn't as tall, dark, handsome and rich as Kirsty had prepared herself for, but... Kirsty stood up and took a deep breath. She was going to lose Ian if she didn't do something about it. Maybe it was time she wrote her own plot. She *would* go to the ball. She would find Ian Fraser and she would tell him exactly how she felt.

What if he rejected her? In a public place? It would be more embarrassing than wearing a placard advertising the fact that she was still a virgin at twenty-four. Kirsty took another calming, deep breath. No, it wouldn't. She would be in disguise. Only Ian would know who she was. That was, if her costume was as good as the hire shop's photographic catalogue had led her to believe.

Kirsty rummaged quickly through the large bag and

extracted the pot of green face paint she had purchased. She stood in front of the bathroom mirror and applied a thick layer. Black eyeliner and lipstick added a dramatic contrast. Kirsty used the eyeliner to black out one of her front teeth as well. She hoped the effect would last. She threw on the shapeless black dress that trailed on the floor and then shook the final items out of the bag. The skin glue made attaching the large, hooked plastic nose to her face quite simple and Kirsty stretched her black lips into a grin as she admired the wart, complete with long black hairs, that protruded from the side of the nose. Then it was time for the finishing touch. In the shop she had had the choice of two wigs, one wispy and white, the other black with long, frizzy curls, and had chosen the black one. She crammed the pointed black hat on top of the wig and grabbed the broomstick.

She was unrecognisable. Incognito. Even if Ian rejected her in front of hundreds of people she wouldn't feel humiliated. She could deny everything and nobody would be sure enough to convict her. And maybe he wouldn't reject her. Kirsty's optimism grew as she gathered up the folds of the black dress and ran lightly down the stairs.

The security guard at the main door let her pass with a grin and a request not to turn him into a toad.

'Too late!' Kirsty grinned back over her shoulder. 'You'll have to wait for a princess.'

The double doors of the gymnasium had been transformed. Heavy black curtains were draped across them, leaving a small V-shaped opening to enter the ball. Ghosts had been made with helium balloons beneath Jane's sheets and they had been cleverly pinned to appear to hold the opening of the curtains. Mounds of earth lay on each side of the door, three-dimensional cardboard tombstones listing at drunken angles. Nobody was left at the door to collect her ticket.

The ball had been in progress for two hours and the gymnasium was rocking. The live band, giving an excellent rendition of 'Rock Around The Clock' made Kirsty's spirits lift. This was *great*! She ducked her head so that the point of her hat wouldn't catch on the black curtains. Then she stood, overwhelmed by the spectacle. It was not going to be as easy as she had hoped to find Ian Fraser.

For a start, the gymnasium was dark. The candles in the Jack-o-lanterns dotted tables around the edge of the vast room, illuminating groups of people in avid conversation and black-covered tables cluttered with glasses and snack-food packets. A laser light show was in progress, the beams of colour cross-hatching what looked like a sea of joyous movement. 'Rock Around The Clock' was being appreciated enthusiastically. Not that there was much room for dancing. The place was packed and Kirsty could see absolutely nobody she could recognise. The costumes were fantastic! Kirsty simply stood near the door, trying to adjust to the sound level, the lighting, and the feeling of being in a totally alien environment.

Witches, ghosts, devils and skeletons were popular choices but the variety was endless. A Fred and Wilma Flintstone were dancing near Kirsty. The soft, over-the-head masks they wore obliterated their identity completely, but Kirsty damped down her twinge of anxiety. Ian was going to be Frankenstein and even if he was wearing a mask she would be able to recognise him once she got close enough. The reminder of why she had come prompted Kirsty to start edging her way further into the party.

Her broom was rather a nuisance. The bristles caught on the multi-coloured wig of a clown. Kirsty shouted an apology over the music. The clown grinned and the red nose came closer.

'Who are you?' the clown asked.

'Kirsty,' she replied loudly. 'Cardiology.'

One of the clown's companions stopped dancing. 'Kirsty? Hi, it's me—Crystal.'

Kirsty laughed. 'Great costume!' Crystal was a gypsy. Brightly coloured scarves were tied around her dark hair. Big gold rings dangled from her ears.

'This clown is my sister-in-law—Nikki Campbell. She and her husband David have just come back for a visit. From Sydney, Australia.'

'Long way to come.' Kirsty smiled. The clown's partner shook his head.

'Nikki can't resist an opportunity to dress up,' he told Kirsty. 'Even if it means changing hemispheres.'

Kirsty admired the white suit with ruffles and big, brightly coloured spots. 'It was either this or a pumpkin.' Nikki laughed. 'See?' She pulled the edges of the suit to reveal a well-rounded abdomen.

'Congratulations.' Kirsty grinned. 'How far along are you?'

'Six months.'

The music changed to Ritchie Valens' 'La Bamba'. A new surge of energy ran through the dance floor.

'We'd better sit down for a while,' Crystal shouted. 'Come with us, Kirsty.'

Kirsty shook her head. 'I have to find someone. Ian Fraser. Have you seen him?'

'What's he wearing?'

'He's Frankenstein.'

'I saw one a while back,' Nikki's husband, David, told her. 'Up near the bar. In fact, I saw a couple of them.'

'Thanks.' Kirsty beamed. 'I'll get hunting.' She eyed the dinner suit David was wearing. The vampire cloak draped over his shoulder looked like an afterthought. 'Where are your fangs?'

'In his pocket,' Crystal shouted. 'Come on, David. Get them out.'

Kirsty left them arguing about whether David should wear his plastic fangs.

'Stick 'em up!' a voice told her firmly.

Kirsty turned to find a plastic tommy-gun pointed at her. The couple dressed as Bonnie and Clyde had glasses in their hands and were obviously enjoying themselves. They wore matching pinstriped suit jackets, Bonnie in a mini-skirt and Clyde in wide trousers. Kirsty looked more closely.

'Josie!' she cried in delight. 'Great. Someone I can recognise.'

'Kirsty?' Josie asked dubiously. 'Is that you?'

Kirsty nodded happily. Her disguise was as good as she'd hoped. Even Josie who saw her almost every day in the staff quarters hadn't recognised her.

'I wouldn't have guessed,' Josie assured her. 'It's only your accent that gives you away. Isn't this fabulous?'

Kirsty nodded. 'Josie, have you seen Ian?'

'I've got no idea. Half the fun is trying to sort out who's who. Some of them won't confess.' Josie looked at Kirsty's empty hand. 'Why don't you get a drink? The bar's up near the stage where the band is.'

'No. I want to find Ian first.'

Josie laughed. 'Good luck!'

Why was she laughing? Was it *that* difficult to find anyone? Kirsty passed a cow, in a wonderful white suit with black splotches. A plastic udder was displayed prominently on the front at stomach level and a girl dressed as Pocahontas was shrieking with delight as she pulled on the teats. Kirsty hurried past. The bar must have been doing a roaring trade.

A swirling cape, black with a crimson lining, caught her eye as the band started a Beach Boy medley with 'Good Vibrations'. One of the three musketeers, the tall figure was perfect for the costume. The hat sported a glamorous ostrich feather that side-swiped Kirsty's hat. The pencil-thin moustache curled seductively over the man's cheeks, almost reaching his dark eyes. Very dark eyes.

'Paolo!' Kirsty gasped.

He hadn't heard her. He was bending towards his partner—a blonde with the longest legs Kirsty had ever seen. The impression was heightened by her French maid costume. The tiny black skirt was short enough to expose the frills of her knickers. The apron was the size of a handkerchief and the frilly garter matched the bunch of lace fastened to the waterfall of blonde curls. It had to be Chantelle. Kirsty shrugged and grinned. At least Paolo wasn't pining. And he hadn't recognised her.

Kirsty got a fright as a witch-doctor rattled his bones as she edged past another group of dancers. His skull mask with a halo of coloured feathers was very effective. He was with another clown and…Frankenstein.

'Ian!' Kirsty shouted. 'Hi! It's me—Kirsty!'

He *was* wearing a mask, with a crew cut of black hair, a gruesome scar across the forehead and large bolts coming from beneath the ears. He pushed the mask up.

'I'm cooking in here,' he told Kirsty. 'And I can't hear very well. What did you say your name was?'

It wasn't Ian. Kirsty vaguely recognised the young man and placed him amongst the laboratory staff where she had delivered blood samples on occasions. 'I'm just a witch,' Kirsty said. 'Are you the only Frankenstein?'

'No way! We're thinking of starting a club. I've found at least ten so far.'

'Oh, no!' Kirsty's anxiety wasn't going to be so easy to dispel this time. She moved on, feeling steadily warmer under the green face paint. She *had* to find Ian. Kirsty tried to move more quickly. A monk stood on her foot and another Dracula leered at her. Kirsty managed to get to the outside of the dancers and began to negotiate the chairs that marked the edge of the table area. The tables were popular, the chairs all filled with many others standing close by. Loud conversations were going on, everything having to be repeated but nobody seeming irritated by the difficulty in communication.

The band stopped at the end of the Beach Boy medley. 'We'll take a short break,' the lead singer announced into the microphone. 'Here's something for all those of you who feel romantically inclined.'

A cheer went up as the recorded version of 'It's Only Make Believe' began. The atmosphere changed dramatically. The lighting became softer and the dancing slowed until there was just a gentle swaying movement of couples in each other's arms. Kirsty felt a new sense of urgency. What if Ian was out there with Heidi? She scanned the floor anxiously looking for a ghost with a large plastic chain. There were ghosts everywhere. One was standing talking to someone in magnificent Highland dress. He wore a huge wig of ginger hair, with a matching beard, moustache and eyebrows. A tartan beret on the wig matched his kilt and he even carried a set of bagpipes under his arm. Ian should have thought of that, Kirsty decided. It would have been much more original than Frankenstein. The number of ghosts was amazing. Perhaps all those who hadn't had the time or imagination to come up with anything else had raided more of Lizzie's linen cupboards for white sheets and cut holes for eyes. No doubt there would be an irate memo from Mrs Imogen Drew in the next few days regarding the number of sheets requiring mending.

Kirsty spotted Charles Bruce. She had expected him to come as Father Christmas but his appearance as Caesar was just as inspired. A gold-leaf headband sat in his white, bushy hair. Gold armbands matched the shoulder sash over the white tunic. Kirsty waved her broom but didn't stop to identify herself. She had caught a glimpse of another Frankenstein on the other side of the dance floor. Two of them!

Kirsty began to edge through the swaying couples, apologising frequently as her broom got in the way. The bristles caught on a Tinkerbell's wings and the handle tangled with a pirate's sword. Another witch, this time with the wispy grey wig, yelled 'Snap!' as Kirsty passed. Several ghosts were rattling plastic chains and howling mournfully as Kirsty neared her destination but she didn't spare them more than a glance. This Frankenstein was the right height and build but he was making a move to go onto the dance floor as the band started up again with 'Shake, Rattle and Roll'. Kirsty grabbed his arm.

'Ian? I've got to talk to you.'

'You've got the wrong monster, lady. I'm Michael.'

'Sorry.' Kirsty backed off hurriedly. His partner, in a black cat costume, was glaring at her.

Kirsty stood still again, a quiet despair accumulating within her. There must be over two hundred people here. Probably a dozen Frankensteins and no way of finding anybody with ease. She would have to wait until after the ball and heaven only knew when that would be. Rumour had it that the more successful staff association functions went on until dawn. If Ian Fraser was here, establishing a relationship with Heidi, then that was far too long to wait.

Kirsty looked away from the crowd, now bathed in roving spotlights of colour. She looked up at the black and orange streamers, festooned with matching balloons and black silhouettes of bats, as though searching for inspiration from on high. Her gaze slowly shifted to the stage where the lead singer of the band was throwing his microphone from hand to hand during an instrumental break.

A stage. A microphone.

Inspiration struck but could she do it? Kirsty felt a trickle of perspiration run down her back which she knew was due to fear rather than the increasing warmth of the gathering. Paolo had considered the venue the perfect occasion for a public announcement.

What if she was to…?

Chapter Ten

KIRSTY didn't give herself time to think.

It would be too easy to chicken out. This was the only opportunity she was likely to get. She cut an urgent trail through the dancers and didn't hesitate when she reached the steps of the stage.

The lead singer of the band looked startled as the green-faced witch swept onto the stage. Kirsty tugged at his arm and he held his microphone well away as she whispered desperately into his ear. A smile began as he listened and he handed his microphone to Kirsty, signalling the other members of the band. The drummer was the last to stop and some dancers apparently had not noticed the lack of music.

Kirsty cleared her throat nervously. 'I'm sorry to interrupt the music,' she said tentatively. 'This will only take a wee minute.'

Everyone was staring. Even the most inebriated dancers ceased moving and Kirsty looked out over a sea of bizarre and colourful costumes, grinning masks and surprised faces. The witch-doctor rattled his bones. Pockets of conversation continued at the tables but most of those seated were also looking in her direction.

'Don't start singing, for God's sake!' someone called loudly.

Kirsty smiled, embarrassed by the wave of laughter. Must be the cath lab staff, she decided. They had been very vocal about her singing abilities when she had accompanied Harry Wilton for his test. The fact that she had been identified slipped past.

'I'm trying to find Ian,' Kirsty said as the laughter subsided. 'Ian Fraser.' The amplification of her voice by the microphone was nerve-racking. 'It's a bit difficult because there are so many Frankensteins out there.'

A small cheer went up. Perhaps the club had succeeded in becoming established.

'I think he might be avoiding me,' Kirsty continued. 'And I can understand why but there's something I really want him to know.'

She took a deep, rather shaky breath. 'You knew all along that what we had was the real thing, didn't you, Ian? That the friendship we had was so good because we were soul mates. Two halves of a whole. Two sides of the same coin. I didn't think we could become lovers. You felt like too much part of myself. I thought I had to find something different.'

Kirsty's voice became softer but she didn't lose her audience. They were *all* listening now. Even the chatter that had continued around the tables had stopped. The silence was complete. Kirsty's eyes roved over the crowd. She still couldn't see Ian. Was he listening? Was he even *here*?

'I was wrong, Ian,' Kirsty said passionately. 'I love you. I've loved you all along only I didn't recognise that it was the genuine article.' Her voice caught. 'I want to spend the rest of my life with you, Ian…and have a baby with terribly red hair. I came here tonight to propose to you. I know that's not how they do it in the books but I don't care. I've been wrong about too many things and I can't afford to lose you.

'Please, Ian. I can't find you. There are too many

Frankensteins.' Kirsty paused and gave a tiny sniff as she collected herself. The plea was coming from the depths of her soul. 'Would the *real* Frankenstein please come forward?'

Heads turned amongst the crowd, waiting for a sign of movement amongst their number. Who could possibly resist a plea that heartfelt? But nobody moved. A low buzz of murmured conversation broke out and Kirsty caught the sympathetic undertone. A prickle ran down her spine. She had made a fool of herself and at least a few people had recognised her voice if they'd asked her not to sing. Soon everybody would know. Kirsty swallowed hard, trying to will away the sinking sensation which she knew would be replaced at any second by an unbearable level of humiliation.

The low buzz of voices increased and was accompanied by an embarrassed shuffling. Everybody was wondering what they should do. The band members were also looking fidgety. The drummer twirled his sticks in his hands and looked questioningly at the keyboard player. The lead singer took a step towards Kirsty, his hand out, but Kirsty's fingers were still locked around the stem of the microphone. Her brain might be shouting at her to give up and escape but her body was not cooperating.

An excruciating sound suddenly cut through the increasing activity of the crowd. A loud squeal that terminated in an agonised squeak, only to be replaced by another squeal. Kirsty recognised the sound instantly. The squashing of a large, very unwell cat. The tuning of a set of bagpipes. She, and everybody else, turned to stare towards the back of the crowd where the noise was emanating from.

There were too many people. Kirsty craned her neck

but couldn't see exactly what was happening. Had a Frankenstein borrowed the bagpipes by way of a response? Or had the wild Highlander decided it was a merciful way to rescue the party from a very awkward interlude?

The appallingly loud experimental sounds ceased. Kirsty recognised the new squeak as the vigorous squeeze on the airbag to ready it for the start of a real tune. And the tune was recognisable. 'Scotland The Brave.' It *couldn't* be Ian playing! It was wonderful! The rich sound filled the gymnasium, the tune coming out clearly over the low, constant drone of the bass notes that seemed to resonate in Kirsty's bones. It was a sound rooted in history. Incredibly stirring. Totally impossible not to be deeply moved.

A gap appeared in the throng towards the back of the huge room. The lone Highlander stepped into the space. The technician controlling the light show during the evening directed a spotlight onto the figure, sending those around him into shadow. His bagpipes were erect, the pipes standing proudly against the flaming red hair, the light glinting on the engraved silver pieces between the lengths of black pipe. The tartan bag was tucked under his arm. His hands were held forward, the fingers moving skilfully over the holes on the chanter.

Kirsty was transfixed. She watched the wave of movement as the costumed guests moved back, creating a clear path. The Highlander moved forward slowly, stepping calmly in time to the strong beat of 'Scotland The Brave'. Someone started clapping and the involvement caught and spread like wildfire. Kirsty heard the drummer behind her.

'Cool!' he exclaimed. A roll of drumming settled into an accompanying tattoo. The other band members grinned and reached for their instruments. Everybody knew the tune and now the crowd of spectators were not simply observing. They were clapping, singing, stamping—all an enthusiastic part of the extraordinary response to Kirsty's interruption to the evening.

The Highlander made a direct line towards the stage where Kirsty stood. He stopped in front of her, tapping his foot in time to the music as he finished the last few bars. Kirsty stared. Was it...*could* it really be Ian Fraser?

The pipe fell from the mouth hidden in the depths of the bush of ginger beard and moustache. The bagpipes slid from his shoulder as the Highlander threw back his head.

'Och, aye, lassie,' he boomed, in a truly awful attempt at a Scottish accent. 'If ye still want to spend the rest of ye life with me after listening to that wee tune...I'm all yours.'

A cheer went up around the Highlander and grew into a crescendo of relief and delight. The spotlight shifted to Kirsty and she felt the microphone being taken from her fingers.

'He's all yours.' The lead singer gave her a nudge towards the steps. 'What are you waiting for?'

The Highlander had unhooked the elastic holding his extravagant facial hair in place, but Kirsty hadn't needed the removal of the disguise to confirm her recognition. His terrible Scottish accent had been enough. That, and the gaze coming from the brown eyes almost hidden beneath the bushy ginger eyebrows. He was carefully laying his bagpipes onto the stage as Kirsty moved down the steps. And then she was holding Ian's hands, the cheering from the crowd was fading and the band launched into a slow, romantic rendition of Air Supply's 'Making Love Out Of Nothing At All'.

'Lose the nose,' Ian said solemnly, dropping Kirsty's hand. 'I can't kiss a face with an obstacle like that on it.' He grinned. 'Especially when the wart's hairy.'

Kirsty pulled the nose off. She tossed it over her shoulder and threw her arms around Ian's neck. Another cheer went up as their lips made contact but neither Kirsty nor Ian was aware of the applause. The kiss started desperately—a release of the tension and despair that had been building for days. Then it changed. Somehow they drew breath without losing contact. Now the kiss became an exchange, questions and answers that wiped any doubts Kirsty had ever harboured about Ian's ability to arouse a passionate response in her body. *This* was the man she wanted. The *only* one.

The band was playing the final chorus of 'Making Love…' when Ian and Kirsty finally broke their kiss. They were standing in the midst of dancing couples but neither had been aware that the ball had regathered its own momentum. A drum roll announced the end of the romantic interlude and the fast Beach Boys number enticed a new surge onto the dance floor. Ian grabbed Kirsty's hand.

'Let's find somewhere quieter.'

They negotiated their way through the queue at the bar and around a couple of tables. The candles in the Jack-o-lanterns were spluttering and some had gone out. The empty glasses and food packages had multiplied. Someone was going to have a big clearing-up operation to do before long. Ian tugged on Kirsty's hand.

'This way, Kirsty. Quick, before anyone sees us.' Ian

pulled her towards a section of the wall draped with a black curtain like the main entrance. He ducked behind the curtain and Kirsty followed but Ian didn't stop. He was feeling his way along the wall.

'What are you doing?' Kirsty exclaimed.

'Shh. I'm trying to find the handle.' Ian was fiddling with something on the wall but it was too dark for Kirsty to see. Then he seemed to disappear into the wall.

'Ian!' Kirsty squeaked. 'Come back!'

A hand came through the gap and beckoned. Kirsty giggled.

'Oh…' she breathed as she stepped forward cautiously. 'I'd forgotten the swimming pool was beside the gymnasium.'

'That's why we put the curtain up. This was definitely out of bounds.' Ian clicked the door shut, muting the sounds of revelry on the other side of the wall.

'So we shouldn't be here?'

'No.' Ian grinned. 'Fancy a swim?'

'I haven't got a costume.'

'Neither have I.'

Ian and Kirsty stared at each other in the dim light and Kirsty recognised the opportunity Ian had given them. They could turn back time, just a little, and repeat an encounter that Kirsty knew would end quite differently this time.

'I love you, Ian.'

'You've said that before.' Ian looked very serious. 'More than once.'

'I know. But now it's different. I *really* love you.'

'What's made you so sure?'

'Lots of things.' Kirsty's eyes widened. 'Were you really going to go back to New Zealand without me?'

'I don't know,' Ian admitted. 'It was certainly the last thing I *wanted* to do. I hoped it might make things clearer for you. I thought maybe the idea of me disappearing to the other side of the world might make you think about what we would have lost.'

'I was already thinking about it,' Kirsty assured him. 'I was getting desperate. You'd always made it so easy for me to come to you and then you shut yourself away. It was so difficult to say anything.'

'I had to know how important it was to you. How hard you were prepared to try. I knew if the positions were reversed then nothing would have stopped *me*.'

'I thought you'd really had enough of me. And I couldn't blame you.' Kirsty looked at Ian wonderingly. 'You even helped me get a date with Paolo.'

'It was one of the hardest things I'd ever done.'

'You let me go out with him knowing that all he wanted was to get me into bed. And you didn't say anything.'

'I said a few things.'

'But you didn't try to stop me.'

'You had to find out for yourself. If I had told you then how I felt about you, you wouldn't have believed it was what you were looking for.'

'No.' Kirsty smiled wryly. 'I felt too safe with you, Ian. I was only *me*. I wanted to become something more. A...a heroine, I guess.'

'You are a heroine.' Ian smiled. 'That was a very brave thing you did—making a public announcement about how you felt.'

'Someone told me it would be the perfect place to make a public announcement. And I didn't think anyone would recognise me with my green face.'

'I recognised you instantly. You're almost the same

colour you were when you got plastered and threw up all over my room.'

Kirsty smiled. 'I was thinking about that just the other night. When I had dinner with James Fenwick.'

'Must have been some dinner!'

'Mmm. Smoked salmon and snails. And the waiter looked like he was wearing roller blades.' Kirsty smiled again at Ian's serious expression. 'I thought about it because it was like a symbol of how much you cared about me—no matter how awful I was. I was trying to explain to James the reasons why I couldn't possibly marry him.'

'What did you say?'

'What I was trying to say was that I needed someone to share my life with. Someone I was going forward *with*, not towards.'

Ian nodded. He understood. Of course he understood, but he still looked serious.

'Smoked salmon,' he said slowly. 'You've had a taste of the high life, Kirsty. I can't promise I'll ever be able to give it to you.'

'A taste was all I needed. It was enough to show me that there are far more important things in life. I don't care about central heating, Ian. Open fires are fine.'

'Good.' Ian was looking bemused.

'What I liked about James was the feeling of being in a family. I never had that before. But I want my own family. *Our* family. Do you think our baby will have red hair?'

'I'd say the odds are fairly high.' Ian reached out and pulled off Kirsty's black wig. He fluffed up her curls. 'How soon do you want to find out?'

'Not too soon.' Kirsty smiled. 'Let's get married first.'

'I'm not sure if I can propose to you yet,' Ian told her firmly. 'James might have been some sort of father figure, but what about Paolo?'

'I was carried away,' Kirsty confessed. 'By...by...'

'Lust,' Ian supplied.

'Mmm. Purely physical. He's very charming but I don't think he really had any intention of marrying me.'

'Why not?'

'Did you see who he was with tonight?'

'The French maid?'

'I think that was Chantelle. They were in bed together when I rang him last night to break off our engagement.'

'So you were going to break it off before you knew that Chantelle was back on the scene?'

'Of course. I knew what the genuine article was by then.'

'And were you really going to propose to *me* if you'd found me earlier tonight?'

'I kept grabbing Frankensteins. Why didn't you tell me you'd changed your mind?'

'I was going to surprise you. If you hadn't turned up I was going to play my bagpipes outside your bedroom window. In fact, I was planning to play what the band has just started next door.'

'Auld Lang Syne? Is the ball over?'

'We had a curfew.' Ian drew Kirsty closer. 'We're going to be all alone here very soon. No threat of being discovered. Besides, I've only got three weeks left at Lizzie's. What could they do? Fire me? I've got another job to go to—we won't starve.'

'Have you? Where?'

'Dunedin. I'm not due to take it up until the end of

February. And I don't have to. Maybe you'd rather go somewhere else?'

'I'll go anywhere as long as I'm with you,' Kirsty declared. 'Three weeks will give me enough time to work out *my* notice at Lizzie's.'

'We could have an extended honeymoon in Europe.'

'Backpacking?'

'Great idea.'

'Eurorail pass?'

'Perfect.'

'We could get married in Scotland.'

'I could wear a kilt!'

'Aye. And I could finally find out what was underneath it.'

'Do you really want to know?'

'Aye.' Kirsty's eyes glowed. Ian's fingers went to the buckles. The kilt slithered to the tiled floor. Kirsty gurgled with laughter. 'Roadrunner!'

Ian grinned. 'You know what I've always wanted to find out?'

'What?'

'What witches wear under those black dresses.' Ian's hold on Kirsty tightened. The hem of her dress was hoisted and Ian's hand was warm against Kirsty's thigh. She caught her breath and her gaze locked with Ian's.

'Are we going for this swim, or what?'

'Oh... ''or what'', please. I don't think I can wait *any* longer.'

Ian's eyes widened. 'You mean...?'

'I had to wait until things were perfect. Now they are.'

'You mean you're *still* a—'

'Don't *say* it!' Kirsty pressed her fingers hard against

Ian's mouth. 'And anyway, I don't intend to be one for much longer. That is, if you...' The urgent mumble made Kirsty remove her fingers from Ian's lips. 'What did you say, Ian?'

'I said—just try and stop me!'

MILLS & BOON

JANUARY 2010 HARDBACK TITLES

ROMANCE

Untamed Billionaire, Undressed Virgin	Anna Cleary
Pleasure, Pregnancy and a Proposition	Heidi Rice
Exposed: Misbehaving with the Magnate	Kelly Hunter
Pregnant by the Playboy Tycoon	Anne Oliver
The Secret Mistress Arrangement	Kimberly Lang
The Marcolini Blackmail Marriage	Melanie Milburne
Bought: One Night, One Marriage	Natalie Anderson
Confessions of a Millionaire's Mistress	Robyn Grady
Housekeeper at His Beck and Call	Susan Stephens
Public Scandal, Private Mistress	Susan Napier
Surrender to the Playboy Sheikh	Kate Hardy
The Magnate's Indecent Proposal	Ally Blake
His Mistress, His Terms	Trish Wylie
The Boss's Bedroom Agenda	Nicola Marsh
Master of Mallarinka & Hired: His Personal Assistant	Way & Steele
The Lucchesi Bride & Adopted: One Baby	Winters & Oakley
An Italian Affair	Margaret McDonagh
Small Miracles	Jennifer Taylor

HISTORICAL

One Unashamed Night	Sophia James
The Captain's Mysterious Lady	Mary Nichols
The Major and the Pickpocket	Lucy Ashford

MEDICAL

A Winter Bride	Meredith Webber
A Dedicated Lady	Gill Sanderson
An Unexpected Choice	Alison Roberts
Nice And Easy	Josie Metcalfe

JANUARY 2010 LARGE PRINT TITLES

ROMANCE

Marchese's Forgotten Bride — Michelle Reid
The Brazilian Millionaire's Love-Child — Anne Mather
Powerful Greek, Unworldly Wife — Sarah Morgan
The Virgin Secretary's Impossible Boss — Carole Mortimer
Claimed: Secret Royal Son — Marion Lennox
Expecting Miracle Twins — Barbara Hannay
A Trip with the Tycoon — Nicola Marsh
Invitation to the Boss's Ball — Fiona Harper

HISTORICAL

The Piratical Miss Ravenhurst — Louise Allen
His Forbidden Liaison — Joanna Maitland
An Innocent Debutante in Hanover Square — Anne Herries

MEDICAL™

The Valtieri Marriage Deal — Caroline Anderson
The Rebel and the Baby Doctor — Joanna Neil
The Country Doctor's Daughter — Gill Sanderson
Surgeon Boss, Bachelor Dad — Lucy Clark
The Greek Doctor's Proposal — Molly Evans
Single Father: Wife and Mother Wanted — Sharon Archer

MILLS & BOON

FEBRUARY 2010 HARDBACK TITLES

ROMANCE

At the Boss's Beck and Call	Anna Cleary
Hot-Shot Tycoon, Indecent Proposal	Heidi Rice
Revealed: A Prince and A Pregnancy	Kelly Hunter
Hot Boss, Wicked Nights	Anne Oliver
The Millionaire's Misbehaving Mistress	Kimberly Lang
Between the Italian's Sheets	Natalie Anderson
Naughty Nights in the Millionaire's Mansion	Robyn Grady
Sheikh Boss, Hot Desert Nights	Susan Stephens
Bought: One Damsel in Distress	Lucy King
The Billionaire's Bought Mistress	Annie West
Playboy Boss, Pregnancy of Passion	Kate Hardy
A Night with the Society Playboy	Ally Blake
One Night with the Rebel Billionaire	Trish Wylie
Two Weeks in the Magnate's Bed	Nicola Marsh
Magnate's Mistress…Accidentally Pregnant	Kimberly Lang
Desert Prince, Blackmailed Bride	Kim Lawrence
The Nurse's Baby Miracle	Janice Lynn
Second Lover	Gill Sanderson

HISTORICAL

The Rake and the Heiress	Marguerite Kaye
Wicked Captain, Wayward Wife	Sarah Mallory
The Pirate's Willing Captive	Anne Herries

MEDICAL™

Angel's Christmas	Caroline Anderson
Someone To Trust	Jennifer Taylor
Morrison's Magic	Abigail Gordon
Wedding Bells	Meredith Webber

0110 Gen Std LP

MILLS & BOON

FEBRUARY 2010 LARGE PRINT TITLES

ROMANCE

Desert Prince, Bride of Innocence	Lynne Graham
Raffaele: Taming His Tempestuous Virgin	Sandra Marton
The Italian Billionaire's Secretary Mistress	Sharon Kendrick
Bride, Bought and Paid For	Helen Bianchin
Betrothed: To the People's Prince	Marion Lennox
The Bridesmaid's Baby	Barbara Hannay
The Greek's Long-Lost Son	Rebecca Winters
His Housekeeper Bride	Melissa James

HISTORICAL

The Brigadier's Daughter	Catherine March
The Wicked Baron	Sarah Mallory
His Runaway Maiden	June Francis

MEDICAL™

Emergency: Wife Lost and Found	Carol Marinelli
A Special Kind of Family	Marion Lennox
Hot-Shot Surgeon, Cinderella Bride	Alison Roberts
A Summer Wedding at Willowmere	Abigail Gordon
Miracle: Twin Babies	Fiona Lowe
The Playboy Doctor Claims His Bride	Janice Lynn

millsandboon.co.uk Community

Join Us!

The Community is the perfect place to meet and chat to kindred spirits who love books and reading as much as you do, but it's also the place to:

- **Get the inside scoop from authors about their latest books**
- **Learn how to write a romance book with advice from our editors**
- **Help us to continue publishing the best in women's fiction**
- **Share your thoughts on the books we publish**
- **Befriend other users**

Forums: Interact with each other as well as authors, editors and a whole host of other users worldwide.

Blogs: Every registered community member has their own blog to tell the world what they're up to and what's on their mind.

Book Challenge: We're aiming to read 5,000 books and have joined forces with The Reading Agency in our inaugural Book Challenge.

Profile Page: Showcase yourself and keep a record of your recent community activity.

Social Networking: We've added buttons at the end of every post to share via digg, Facebook, Google, Yahoo, technorati and de.licio.us.

www.millsandboon.co.uk

0909/COMMUNITY HB